Italian

HENRY JAMES

Italian Tales

ZULMA
classics

ZULMA
classics

JANE AUSTEN
Northanger Abbey
and Love and Freindship

WILKIE COLLINS
The Haunted Hotel
and The Dream-Woman

THOMAS HARDY
The Well-Beloved
and Alicia's Diary

NATHANIEL HAWTHORNE
Lady Eleanore's Mantle
and Other Tales of Mystery

HENRY JAMES
Italian Tales

SHERIDAN LE FANU
Carmilla

ROBERT LOUIS STEVENSON
Strange Case of Dr. Jekyll and Mr. Hyde
and Essays in the Art of Writing

OSCAR WILDE
The Picture of Dorian Gray
and The Decay of Lying

∽∾∾

Typeset in Minion and Bauer Bodoni.
Cover design: David Lee Fong.
Cover painting: *Una brisa de recuerdos*, by Raúl Agrán (Picture Alain Mangin).
Printed in France.

ISBN 2-84304-287-9

CONTENTS

CONTENTS

FOREWORD

JAMES is the most European of the American writers. His lifelong fascination with Italy follows a literary tradition introduced by Shakespeare, Goethe and Stendhal, and closer to his time George Sand, Ruskin and Henri de Régnier. From his first taste of the country aged 27, in 1870, to his last visit in 1907, nine years before his death, James spent both short and prolonged stays in Italy, with a particular penchant for Venice and Florence, and to a lesser extent Rome and Naples.

Travelling Companions was written on James' return to America in 1870, full of nostalgia for Italy; it is set in the places he visited. Told in the first person like the other two stories in this collection, it recounts the narrator's encounters with a young American girl travelling with her father. The two young people bump into each other in each new town they visit. James explores all the "irregularities of the heart"—the misunderstandings, suspicions and silences that are his speciality, but for once he creates a happy ending.

Such is not the case with *The Diary of a Man of Fifty*, written at a later date—1879—when James had just published his first major novel *Roderick Hudson*. In *Travelling Companions*, Charlotte Evans likens Italy to a "bewitching novel;" the former soldier narrating this story confides to his diary his irresistible urge to return to Florence, site of a previous love affair, after an absence of twenty-seven years. There he meets a young man in love with a countess, the daughter of the very countess he used to love so desperately. The narrator sees in this young man a kind of double of the man he used to be, and attempts to put him on his guard. The themes of repetition and ambiguity suggest that the Jamesian enigmas of later tales—from *The Private Life* and *The Wheel of Time* to *The Turn of the Screw*—could well have originated in this short story.

However Venice is the most disturbing city of all; Venice, where the Bordereau ladies, Tina and her aunt Juliana, live like hermits in an ancient palace. Juliana was, a very long time ago, the poet Jeffrey Aspern's muse; she has in her possession some key papers— letters and documents—that she insists on keeping to herself. The narrator, a passionate Aspern specialist, takes lodgings at Juliana's house as part of a complex strategy for getting hold of the precious papers. This tale was told to James in almost identical form save that it took place in Florence, and the poet in question was none other than Byron. The story, published with *The Turn of the Screw* in 1888, is a sort of mystery behind closed doors, its enigmatic thrusts and withdrawals mirroring the character of Tina, the niece, who gives too much away at the same time as she tries to protect herself. None of the three characters emerge from the supposedly innocent games unscathed, with the tragedy creeping up on the reader until the moment of no return, when the conclusion becomes inevitable. This is a delightful evocation of the love of literature; each time Juliana appears the narrator sees in her the woman the poet loved, her voice is the voice he heard. It is also a passionate hymn to the dark yet golden city of Venice. In the preface to *The Aspern Papers* James writes of Italy "stretching beyond our ken and escaping our penetration;" such is the mystery of life and literature, and such is the delight of James, who improves on each re-reading.

Travelling Companions was published in the *Atlantic Monthly* in 1870. *The Diary of a Man of Fifty* was serialized both in *Harper's New Monthly Magazine* and *Macmillan's Magazine* before it was published in *The Madonna of the Future and Other Tales* (Macmillan, 1879). *The Aspern Papers* was serialized in the *Atlantic Monthly* before it was published in *The Aspern Papers* (Macmillan, 1888). It was later entirely revised by James, and this new text published in the New York Edition of his *Novels and Tales* (Scribner's, 1907-1909). The texts reproduced here are those of the last editions published and revised by Henry James himself. A few errors in spelling and punctuation have been silently corrected.

The Aspern Papers

I

I HAD taken Mrs. Prest into my confidence; without her in truth I should have made but little advance, for the fruitful idea in the whole business dropped from her friendly lips. It was she who found the short cut and loosed the Gordian knot. It is not supposed easy for women to rise to the large free view of anything, anything to be done; but they sometimes throw off a bold conception—such as a man wouldn't have risen to—with singular serenity. "Simply make them take you in on the footing of a lodger"—I don't think that unaided I should have risen to that. I was beating about the bush, trying to be ingenious, wondering by what combination of arts I might become an acquaintance, when she offered this happy suggestion that the way to become an acquaintance was first to become an intimate. Her actual knowledge of the Misses Bordereau was scarcely larger than mine, and indeed I had brought with me from England some definite facts that were new to her. Their name had been mixed up ages before with one of the greatest names of the century, and they now lived obscurely in Venice, lived on very small means, unvisited, unapproachable, in a sequestered and dilapidated old palace: this was the substance of my friend's impression of them. She herself had been established in Venice some fifteen years and had done a great deal of good there; but the circle of her benevolence had never embraced the two shy, mysterious and, as was somehow supposed, scarcely respectable Americans—they were believed to have lost in their long exile all national quality, besides being as their name implied of some remoter French affiliation—who asked no favours and desired no attention. In the early years of her residence she had made an attempt to see them, but this had been successful only as regards the little one, as Mrs. Prest called the niece; though in fact I afterwards found her the bigger of the two in inches. She had heard Miss Bordereau was ill and had a suspicion she was in want, and had gone to the house to offer aid, so that if there were suffering, American suffering in particular, she shouldn't have it on her conscience. The "little one" had received her in the great cold tarnished Venetian *sala*, the central hall of the house, paved with marble and roofed with dim cross-beams, and hadn't even asked her to sit down. This was not encouraging for me, who wished to sit so fast, and I remarked as much to Mrs. Prest. She replied, however, with profundity, "Ah, but there's all the difference: I went to confer a favour and you'll go to ask one. If they're proud you'll be on the right side." And she offered to show me their house to begin with—to row me thither in her gondola. I let her know I had already been to look at it half a dozen times; but I accepted her invitation, for it charmed me to hover about the place. I had made my way to it the day after my arrival in Venice—it had been described to me in advance by the friend in England to whom I owed definite information as to their possession of the papers— laying siege to it with my eyes while I considered my plan of campaign. Jeffrey Aspern had never been in it that I knew of, but some note of his voice seemed to abide there by a roundabout implication and in a "dying fall".

Mrs. Prest knew nothing about the papers, but was interested in my curiosity, as always in the joys and sorrows of her friends. As we went, however, in her gondola, gliding there under the sociable hood with the bright Venetian picture framed on either side by the movable window, I saw how my eagerness amused her and that she found my interest in my possible spoil a fine case of monomania. "One would think you expected from it the answer to the riddle of the universe," she said; and I denied the impeachment only by replying that if I had to choose between that precious solution and a bundle of Jeffrey Aspern's letters I knew indeed which would appear to me the greater boon. She pretended to make light of his genius and I took no pains to defend him. One doesn't defend one's god: one's god is in himself a defence. Besides, to-day, after his long comparative obscuration, he hangs high in the heaven of our literature for all the world to see; he's a part of the light by which we walk. The most I said was that he was no doubt not a woman's poet; to which she rejoined aptly enough that he had been at least Miss Bordereau's. The strange thing had been for me to discover in England that she was still alive: it was as if I had been told Mrs. Siddons was, or Queen Caroline, or the famous Lady Hamilton, for it seemed to me that she belonged to a generation as extinct. "Why, she must be tremendously old—at least a hundred," I had said; but on coming to consider dates I saw it not strictly involved that she should have far exceeded the common span. None the less she was of venerable age and her relations with Jeffrey Aspern had occurred in her early womanhood. "That's her excuse," said Mrs. Prest half-sententiously and yet also somewhat as if she were ashamed of making a speech so little in the real tone of Venice. As if a woman needed an excuse for having loved the divine poet! He had been not only one of the most brilliant minds of his day—and in those years, when the century was young, there were, as every one knows, many—but one of the most genial men and one of the handsomest.

The niece, according to Mrs. Prest, was of minor antiquity, and the conjecture was risked that she was only a grand-niece. This was possible; I had nothing but my share in the very limited knowledge of my English fellow worshipper John Cumnor, who had never seen the couple. The world, as I say, had recognised Jeffrey Aspern, but Cumnor and I had recognised him most. The multitude to-day flocked to his temple, but of that temple he and I regarded our-selves as the appointed ministers. We held, justly, as I think, that we had done more for his memory than any one else, and had done it simply by opening lights into his life. He had nothing to fear from us because he had nothing to fear from the truth, which alone at such a distance of time we could be interested in establishing. His early death had been the only dark spot, as it were, on his fame, unless the papers in Miss Bordereau's hands should perversely bring out others. There had been an impression about 1825 that he had "treated her badly," just as there had been an impression that he had "served," as the London populace says, several other ladies in the same masterful way. Each of these cases Cumnor and I had been able to investigate, and we had never failed to acquit him conscientiously of any grossness. I judged him perhaps more indulgently than my friend; certainly, at any rate, it appeared to me

that no man could have walked straighter in the given circumstances. These had been almost always difficult and dangerous.
Half the women of his time, to speak liberally, had flung themselves at his head, and while the fury raged—the more that it was
very catching—accidents, some of them grave, had not failed to
occur. He was not a woman's poet, as I had said to Mrs. Prest, in
the modern phase of his reputation; but the situation had been
different when the man's own voice was mingled with his song.
That voice, by every testimony, was one of the most charming ever
heard. "Orpheus and the Maenads!" had been of course my foreseen judgement when I first turned over his correspondence.
Almost all the Maenads were unreasonable and many of them
unbearable; it struck me that he had been kinder and more con-
siderate than in his place—if I could imagine myself in any such
box—I should have found the trick of.

It was certainly strange beyond all strangeness, and I shall not
take up space with attempting to explain it, that whereas among all
these other relations and in these other directions of research we
had to deal with phantoms and dust, the mere echoes of echoes,
the one living source of information that had lingered on into our
time had been unheeded by us. Every one of Aspern's contemporaries had, according to our belief, passed away; we had not been
able to look into a single pair of eyes into which his had looked
or to feel a transmitted contact in any aged hand that his had
touched. Most dead of all did poor Miss Bordereau appear, and yet
she alone had survived. We exhausted in the course of months our
wonder that we had not found her out sooner, and the substance
of our explanation was that she had kept so quiet. The poor lady
on the whole had had reason for doing so. But it was a revelation to
us that self-effacement on such a scale had been possible in the
latter half of the nineteenth century—the age of newspapers and
telegrams and photographs and interviewers. She had taken no
great trouble for it either—hadn't hidden herself away in an undis-
coverable hole, had boldly settled down in a city of exhibition. The
one apparent secret of her safety had been that Venice contained so
many much greater curiosities. And then accident had somehow
favoured her, as was shown for example in the fact that Mrs. Prest

had never happened to name her to me, though I had spent three weeks in Venice—under her nose, as it were—five years before. My friend indeed had not named her much to any one; she appeared almost to have forgotten the fact of her continuance. Of course Mrs. Prest hadn't the nerves of an editor. It was meanwhile no explanation of the old woman's having eluded us to say that she lived abroad, for our researches had again and again taken us—not only by correspondence but by personal inquiry—to France, to Germany, to Italy, in which countries, not counting his important stay in England, so many of the too few years of Aspern's career had been spent. We were glad to think at least that in all our promulgations—some people now consider I believe that we have overdone them—we had only touched in passing and in the most discreet manner on Miss Bordereau's connection. Oddly enough, even if we had had the material—and we had often wondered what could have become of it—this would have been the most difficult episode to handle.

The gondola stopped, the old palace was there; it was a house of the class which in Venice carries even in extreme dilapidation the dignified name. "How charming! It's grey and pink!" my companion exclaimed; and that is the most comprehensive description of it. It was not particularly old, only two or three centuries; and it had an air not so much of decay as of quiet discouragement, as if it had rather missed its career. But its wide front, with a stone balcony from end to end of the *piano nobile* or most important floor, was architectural enough, with the aid of various pilasters and arches; and the stucco with which in the intervals it had long ago been endued was rosy in the April afternoon. It overlooked a clean melancholy rather lonely canal, which had a narrow *riva* or convenient footway on either side. "I don't know why—there are no brick gables," said Mrs. Prest, "but this corner has seemed to me before more Dutch than Italian, more like Amsterdam than like Venice. It's eccentrically neat, for reasons of its own; and though you may pass on foot scarcely any one ever thinks of doing so. It's as negative—considering *where* it is—as a Protestant Sunday. Perhaps the people are afraid of the Misses Bordereau. I daresay they have the reputation of witches."

I forget what answer I made to this—I was given up to two other reflexions. The first of these was that if the old lady lived in such a big and imposing house she couldn't be in any sort of misery and therefore wouldn't be tempted by a chance to let a couple of rooms. I expressed this fear to Mrs. Prest, who gave me a very straight answer. "If she didn't live in a big house how could it be a question of her having rooms to spare? If she were not amply lodged you'd lack ground to approach her. Besides, a big house here, and especially in this *quartier perdu*, proves nothing at all: it's perfectly consistent with a state of penury. Dilapidated old *palazzi*, if you'll go out of the way for them, are to be had for five shillings a year. And as for the people who live in them—no, until you've explored Venice socially as much as I have, you can form no idea of their domestic desolation. They live on nothing, for they've nothing to live on." The other idea that had come into my head was connected with a high blank wall which appeared to confine an expanse of ground on one side of the house. Blank I call it, but it was figured over with the patches that please a painter, repaired breaches, crumblings of plaster, extrusions of brick that had turned pink with time; while a few thin trees, with the poles of certain rickety trellises, were visible over the top. The place was a garden and apparently attached to the house. I suddenly felt that so attached it gave me my pretext.

I sat looking out on all this with Mrs. Prest (it was covered with the golden glow of Venice) from the shade of our *felze*, and she asked me if I would go in then, while she waited for me, or come back another time. At first I couldn't decide—it was doubtless very weak of me. I wanted still to think I *might* get a footing, and was afraid to meet failure, for it would leave me, as I remarked to my companion, without another arrow for my bow. "Why not another?" she inquired as I sat there hesitating and thinking it over; and she wished to know why even now and before taking the trouble of becoming an inmate—which might be wretchedly uncomfortable after all, even if it succeeded—I hadn't the resource of simply offering them a sum of money down. In that way I might get what I wanted without bad nights.

"Dearest lady," I exclaimed, "excuse the impatience of my tone when I suggest that you must have forgotten the very fact—surely I communicated it to you—which threw me on your ingenuity. The old woman won't have her relics and tokens so much as spoken of; they're personal, delicate, intimate, and she hasn't the feelings of the day, God bless her! If I should sound that note first I should certainly spoil the game. I can arrive at my spoils only by putting her off her guard, and I can put her off her guard only by ingratiating diplomatic arts. Hypocrisy, duplicity are my only chance. I'm sorry for it, but there's no baseness I wouldn't commit for Jeffrey Aspern's sake. First I must take tea with her—then tackle the main job." And I told over what had happened to John Cumnor on his respectfully writing to her. No notice whatever had been taken of his first letter, and the second had been answered very sharply, in six lines, by the niece. "Miss Bordereau requested her to say that she couldn't imagine what he meant by troubling them. They had none of Mr. Aspern's 'literary remains,' and if they *had* had wouldn't have dreamed of showing them to any one on any account whatever. She couldn't imagine what he was talking about and begged he would let her alone." I certainly didn't want to be met that way.

"Well," said Mrs. Prest after a moment and all provokingly, "perhaps they really haven't anything. If they deny it flat how are you sure?"

"John Cumnor's sure, and it would take me long to tell you how his conviction, or his very strong presumption—strong enough to stand against the old lady's not unnatural fib—has built itself up. Besides, he makes much of the internal evidence of the niece's letter."

"The internal evidence?"

"Her calling him 'Mr. Aspern.'"

"I don't see what that proves."

"It proves familiarity, and familiarity implies the possession of mementoes, of tangible objects. I can't tell you how that 'Mr.' affects me—how it bridges over the gulf of time and brings our hero near to me—nor what an edge it gives to my desire to see Juliana. You don't say 'Mr.' Shakespeare."

"Would I, any more, if I had a box full of his letters?"

"Yes, if he had been your lover and some one wanted them."
And I added that John Cumnor was so convinced, and so all the
more convinced by Miss Bordereau's tone, that he would have
come himself to Venice on the undertaking were it not for the
obstacle of his having, for any confidence, to disprove his identity
with the person who had written to them, which the old ladies
would be sure to suspect in spite of dissimulation and a change of
name. If they were to ask him point-blank if he were not their
snubbed correspondent it would be too awkward for him to lie;
whereas I was fortunately not tied in that way. I was a fresh hand—
I could protest without lying.

"But you'll have to take a false name," said Mrs. Prest. "Juliana
lives out of the world as much as it is possible to live, but she has
none the less probably heard of Mr. Aspern's editors. She perhaps
possesses what you've published."

"I've thought of that," I returned; and I drew out of my pocket-
book a visiting-card neatly engraved with a well-chosen *nom de
guerre*.

"You're very extravagant—it adds to your immorality. You
might have done it in pencil or ink," said my companion.

"This looks more genuine."

"Certainly you've the courage of your curiosity. But it will be
awkward about your letters; they won't come to you in that mask."

"My banker will take them in and I shall go every day to get
them. It will give me a little walk."

"Shall you depend all on that?" asked Mrs. Prest. "Aren't you
coming to see me?"

"Oh, you'll have left Venice for the hot months long before
there are any results. I'm prepared to roast all summer—as well as
through the long hereafter perhaps you'll say! Meanwhile John
Cumnor will bombard me with letters addressed, in my feigned
name, to the care of the *padrona*."

"She'll recognise his hand," my companion suggested.

"On the envelope he can disguise it."

"Well, you're a precious pair! Doesn't it occur to you that even
if you're able to say you're not Mr. Cumnor in person they may still
suspect you of being his emissary?"

"Certainly, and I see only one way to parry that."

"And what may that be?"

I hesitated a moment. "To make love to the niece."

"Ah," cried Mrs. Prest, "wait till you see her!"

II

"I MUST work the garden—I must work the garden," I said to myself five minutes later and while I waited, upstairs, in the long, dusky *sala*, where the bare scagliola floor gleamed vaguely in a chink of the closed shutters. The place was impressive, yet looked somehow cold and cautious. Mrs. Prest had floated away, giving me a rendezvous at the end of half an hour by some neighbouring water-steps; and I had been let into the house, after pulling the rusty bell-wire, by a small red-headed and white-faced maid-servant, who was very young and not ugly and wore clicking pattens and a shawl in the fashion of a hood. She had not contented herself with opening the door from above by the usual arrangement of a creaking pulley, though she had looked down at me first from an upper window, dropping the cautious challenge which in Italy precedes the act of admission. I was irritated as a general thing by this survival of medieval manners, though as so fond, if yet so special, an antiquarian I suppose I ought to have liked it; but, with my resolve to be genial from the threshold at any price, I took my false card out of my pocket and held it up to her, smiling as if it were a magic token. It had the effect of one indeed, for it brought her, as I say, all the way down. I begged her to hand it to her mistress, having first written on it in Italian the words: "Could you very kindly see a gentleman, a travelling American, for a moment?" The little maid wasn't hostile—even that was perhaps something gained. She coloured, she smiled and looked both frightened and pleased. I could see that my arrival was a great affair, that visits in such a house were rare and that she was a person who would have liked a bustling place. When she pushed forward the heavy door behind me I felt my foot in the citadel and promised myself ever so firmly to keep it there. She pattered across the damp stony lower hall and I followed her up the high stair-case—stonier still, as it seemed—without an invitation. I think she had meant I should wait for her below, but such was not my idea, and I took up my station in the *sala*. She flitted, at the far end of it, into impenetrable regions, and I looked at the place with my heart beating as I had known it to do in dentists' parlours. It had a gloomy grandeur, but owed its character almost all to its noble shape and to the fine architectural doors, as high as those of grand frontages, which, leading into the various rooms, repeated them-selves on either side at intervals. They were surmounted with old faded painted escutcheons, and here and there in the spaces between them hung brown pictures, which I noted as speciously bad, in battered and tarnished frames that were yet more desirable than the canvases themselves. With the exception of several straw-bottomed chairs that kept their backs to the wall the grand obscure vista contained little else to minister to effect. It was evidently never used save as a passage, and scantly even as that. I may add that by the time the door through which the maid-servant had escaped opened again my eyes had grown used to the want of light.

I hadn't meanwhile meant by my private ejaculation that I must myself cultivate the soil of the tangled enclosure which lay beneath the windows, but the lady who came toward me from the distance over the hard shining floor might have supposed as much from the way in which, as I went rapidly to meet her, I exclaimed, taking care to speak Italian: "The garden, the garden—do me the pleasure to tell me if it's yours!"

She stopped short, looking at me with wonder; and then, "Nothing here is mine," she answered in English, coldly and sadly.

"Oh, you're English; how delightful!" I ingenuously cried. "But surely the garden belongs to the house?"

"Yes, but the house doesn't belong to me." She was a long lean pale person, habited apparently in a dull-coloured dressing-gown, and she spoke very simply and mildly. She didn't ask me to sit down, any more than years before—if she were the niece—she had asked Mrs. Prest, and we stood face to face in the empty pompous hall.

"Well, then, would you kindly tell me to whom I must address myself? I'm afraid you'll think me horribly intrusive, but you know I *must* have a garden—upon my honour I must!"

Her face was not young, but it was candid; it was not fresh, but it was clear. She had large eyes which were not bright, and a great deal of hair which was not "dressed," and long fine hands which were—possibly—not clean. She clasped these members almost convulsively as, with a confused alarmed look, she broke out: "Oh, don't take it away from us; we like it ourselves!"

"You have the use of it then?"

"Oh, yes. If it wasn't for that——!" And she gave a wan vague smile.

"Isn't it a luxury, precisely? That's why, intending to be in Venice some weeks, possibly all summer, and having some literary work, some reading and writing to do, so that I must be quiet and yet if possible a great deal in the open air—that's why I've felt a garden to be really indispensable. I appeal to your own experience," I went on with as sociable a smile as I could risk. "Now can't I look at yours?"

"I don't know, I don't understand," the poor woman murmured, planted there and letting her weak wonder deal —helplessly enough, as I felt—with my strangeness.

"I mean only from one of those windows—such grand ones as you have here—if you'll let me open the shutters." And I walked toward the back of the house. When I had advanced halfway I stopped and waited as in the belief she would accompany me. I had been of necessity quite abrupt, but I strove at the same time to give her the impression of extreme courtesy. "I've looked at furnished rooms all over the place, and it seems impossible to find any with a garden attached. Naturally in a place like Venice gardens are rare. It's absurd if you like, for a man, but I can't live without flowers."

"There are none to speak of down there." She came nearer, as if, though she mistrusted me, I had drawn her by an invisible thread. I went on again, and she continued as she followed me: "We've a few, but they're very common. It costs too much to cultivate them; one has to have a man."

"Why shouldn't I be the man?" I asked. "I'll work without wages; or rather I'll put in a gardener. You shall have the sweetest flowers in Venice."

She protested against this with a small quaver of sound that might have been at the same time a gush of rapture for my free sketch. Then she gasped: "We don't know you—we don't know you."

"You know me as much as I know you; or rather much more, because you know my name. And if you're English I'm almost a countryman."

"We're not English," said my companion, watching me in practical submission while I threw open the shutters of one of the divisions of the wide high window.

"You speak the language so beautifully: might I ask what you are?" Seen from above the garden was in truth shabby, yet I felt at a glance that it had great capabilities. She made no rejoinder, she was so lost in her blankness and gentleness, and I exclaimed: "You don't mean to say you're also by chance American?"

"I don't know. We used to be."

"Used to be? Surely you haven't changed?"

"It's so many years ago. We don't seem to be anything now."

"So many years that you've been living here? Well, I don't wonder at that; it's a grand old house. I suppose you all use the garden," I went on, "but I assure you I shouldn't be in your way. I'd be very quiet and stay quite in one corner."

"We all use it?" she repeated after me vaguely, not coming close to the window but looking at my shoes. She appeared to think me capable of throwing her out.

"I mean all your family—as many as you are."

"There's only one other than me. She's very old. She never goes down."

I feel again my thrill at this close identification of Juliana; in spite of which, however, I kept my head. "Only one other in all this great house!" I feigned to be not only amazed but almost scandalised. "Dear lady, you must have space then to spare!"

"To spare?" she repeated—almost as for the rich unwonted joy to her of spoken words.

"Why you surely don't live (two quiet women—I see *you* are quiet, at any rate) in fifty rooms!" Then with a burst of hope and cheer I put the question straight: "Couldn't you for a good rent *let* me two or three? That would set me up!"

I had now struck the note that translated my purpose, and I needn't reproduce the whole of the tune I played. I ended by making my entertainer believe me an undesigning person, though of course I didn't even attempt to persuade her I was not an eccentric one. I repeated that I had studies to pursue; that I wanted quiet; that I delighted in a garden and had vainly sought one up and down the city: that I would undertake that before another month was over the dear old house should be smothered in flowers. I think it was the flowers that won my suit, for I afterwards found that Miss Tina—for such the name of this high tremulous spinster proved somewhat incongruously to be—had an insatiable appetite for them. When I speak of my suit as won I mean that before I left her she had promised me she would refer the question to her aunt. I invited information as to who her aunt might be and she answered, "Why, Miss Bordereau!" with an air of surprise, as if I might have been expected to know. There were contradictions like this in Miss Tina which, as I observed later, contributed to make her rather pleasingly incalculable and interesting. It was the study of the two ladies to live so that the world shouldn't talk of them or touch them, and yet they had never altogether accepted the idea that it didn't hear of them. In Miss Tina at any rate a grateful susceptibility to human contact had not died out, and contact of a limited order there would be if I should come to live in the house.

"We've never done anything of the sort; we've never had a lodger or any kind of inmate." So much as this she made a point of saying to me. "We're very poor, we live very badly—almost on nothing. The rooms are very bare—those you might take; they've nothing at all in them. I don't know how you'd sleep, how you'd eat."

"With your permission I could easily put in a bed and a few

tables and chairs. *C'est la moindre des choses* and the affair of an hour or two. I know a little man from whom I can hire for a trifle what I should so briefly want, what I should use; my gondolier can bring the things round in his boat. Of course in this great house you must have a second kitchen, and my servant, who's a wonder-fully handy fellow"—this personage was an evocation of the moment—"can easily cook me a chop there. My tastes and habits are of the simplest: I live on flowers!" And then I ventured to add that if they were very poor it was all the more reason they should let their rooms. They were bad economists—I had never heard of such a waste of material.

I saw in a moment my good lady had never before been spoken to in any such fashion—with a humorous firmness that didn't exclude sympathy, that was quite founded on it. She might easily have told me that my sympathy was impertinent, but this by good fortune didn't occur to her. I left her with the understanding that she would submit the question to her aunt and that I might come back the next day for their decision.

"The aunt will refuse; she'll think the whole proceeding very *louche*!" Mrs. Prest declared shortly after this, when I had resumed my place in her gondola. She had put the idea into my head and now—so little are women to be counted on—she appeared to take a despondent view of it. Her pessimism provoked me and I pretended to have the best hopes; I went so far as to boast of a distinct prevision of success. Upon this Mrs. Prest broke out: "Oh, I see what's in your head! You fancy you've made such an impres-sion in five minutes that she's dying for you to come and can be depended on to bring the old one round. If you do get in you'll count it as a triumph."

I did count it as a triumph, but only for the commentator—in the last analysis—not for the man, who had not the tradition of personal conquest. When I went back on the morrow the little maid-servant conducted me straight through the long *sala*—it opened there as before in large perspective and was lighter now, which I thought a good omen—into the apartment from which the recipient of my former visit had emerged on that occasion. It was a spacious, shabby parlour with a fine old painted ceiling under which a strange figure sat alone at one of the windows. They come back to me now almost with the palpitation they caused, the successive states marking my consciousness that as the door of the room closed behind me I was really face to face with the Juliana of some of Aspern's most exquisite and most renowned lyrics. I grew used to her afterwards, though never completely; but as she sat there before me my heart beat as fast as if the miracle of resurrection had taken place for my benefit. Her presence seemed somehow to contain and express his own, and I felt nearer to him at that first moment of seeing her than I ever had been before or ever have been since. Yes, I remember my emotions in their order, even including a curious little tremor that took me when I saw the niece not to be there. With her, the day before, I had become sufficiently familiar, but it almost exceeded my courage—much as I had longed for the event—to be left alone with so terrible a relic as the aunt. She was too strange, too literally resurgent. Then came a check from the perception that we weren't really face to face, inasmuch as she had over her eyes a horrible green shade which served for her almost as a mask. I believed for the instant that she had put it on expressly, so that from underneath it she might take me all in without my getting at herself. At the same time it created a presumption of some ghastly death's-head lurking behind it. The divine Juliana as a grinning skull—the vision hung there until it passed. Then it came to me that she *was* tremendously old—so old that death might take her at any moment, before I should have time to compass my end. The next thought was a correction to that; it lighted up the situation. She would die next week, she would die tomorrow—then I could pounce on her possessions and ransack her drawers. Meanwhile she sat there neither moving nor speaking. She was very small and shrunken, bent forward with her hands in her lap. She was dressed in black and her head was wrapped in a piece of old black lace which showed no hair.

My emotion keeping me silent she spoke first, and the remark she made was exactly the most unexpected.

III

"OUR house is very far from the centre, but the little canal is very *comme il faut.*"

"It's the sweetest corner of Venice and I can imagine nothing more charming," I hastened to reply. The old lady's voice was very thin and weak, but it had an agreeable, cultivated murmur and there was wonder in the thought that that individual note had been in Jeffrey Aspern's ear.

"Please to sit down there. I hear very well," she said quietly, as if perhaps I had been shouting; and the chair she pointed to was at a certain distance. I took possession of it, assuring her I was perfectly aware of my intrusion and of my not having been properly introduced, and that I could but throw myself on her indulgence. Perhaps the other lady, the one I had had the honour of seeing the day before, would have explained to her about the garden. That was literally what had given me courage to take a step so unconventional. I had fallen in love at sight with the whole place—she herself was probably so used to it that she didn't know the impression it was capable of making on a stranger—and I had felt it really a case to risk something. Was her own kindness in receiving me a sign that I was not wholly out in my calculation? It would make me extremely happy to think so. I could give her my word of honour that I was a most respectable inoffensive person and that as a co-tenant of the palace, so to speak, they would be barely conscious of my existence. I would conform to any regulations, any restrictions, if they would only let me enjoy the garden. Moreover I should be delighted to give her references, guarantees; they would be of the very best, both in Venice and in England, as well as in America.

She listened to me in perfect stillness and I felt her look at me with great penetration, though I could see only the lower part of her bleached and shrivelled face. Independently of the refining process of old age it had a delicacy which once must have been great. She had been very fair, she had had a wonderful complexion. She was silent a little after I had ceased speaking; then she began: "If you're so fond of a garden why don't you go to *terra firma,* where there are so many far better than this?"

"Oh, it's the combination!" I answered, smiling; and then with rather a flight of fancy: "It's the idea of a garden in the middle of the sea."

"This isn't the middle of the sea; you can't so much as see the water."

I stared a moment, wondering if she wished to convict me of fraud. "Can't see the water? Why, dear madam, I can come up to the very gate in my boat."

She appeared inconsequent, for she said vaguely in reply to this: "Yes, if you've got a boat. I haven't any; it's many years since I've been in one of the *gondole.*" She uttered these words as if they designed a curious far-away craft known to her only by hearsay.

"Let me assure you of the pleasure with which I would put mine at your service!" I returned. I had scarcely said this, however, before I became aware that the speech was in questionable taste and might also do me the injury of making me appear too eager, too possessed of a hidden motive. But the old woman remained impenetrable and her attitude worried me by suggesting that she had a fuller vision of me than I had of her. She gave me no thanks for my somewhat extravagant offer, but remarked that the lady I had seen the day before was her niece; she would presently come in. She had asked her to stay away a little on purpose—had had her reasons for seeing me first alone. She relapsed into silence and I turned over the fact of these unmentioned reasons and the question of what might come yet; also that of whether I might venture on some judicious remark in praise of her companion. I went so far as to say I should be delighted to see our absent friend again: she had been so very patient with me, considering how odd she must have thought me—a declaration which drew from Miss Bordereau another of her whimsical speeches.

"She has very good manners; I bred her up myself!" I was on the point of saying that that accounted for the easy grace of the niece, but I arrested myself in time, and the next moment the old woman went on: "I don't care who you may be—I don't want to know; it signifies very little to-day." This had all the air of being a formula of dismissal, as if her next words would be that I might take myself off now that she had had the amusement of looking on the face of such a monster of indiscretion. Therefore I was all the more surprised when she added in her soft venerable quaver: "You may have as many rooms as you like—if you'll pay me a good deal of money."

I hesitated but an instant, long enough to measure what she meant in particular by this condition. First it struck me that she must have really a large sum in her mind; then I reasoned quickly that her idea of a large sum would probably not correspond to my own. My deliberation, I think, was not so visible as to diminish the promptitude with which I replied: "I will pay with pleasure and of course in advance whatever you may think it proper to ask me."

"Well, then, a thousand francs a month," she said instantly, while her baffling green shade continued to cover her attitude.

The figure, as they say, was startling and my logic had been at fault. The sum she had mentioned was, by the Venetian measure of such matters, exceedingly large; there was many an old palace in an out-of-the-way corner that I might on such terms have enjoyed the whole of by the year. But so far as my resources allowed I was prepared to spend money, and my decision was quickly taken. I would pay her with a smiling face what she asked, but in that case I would make it up by getting hold of my "spoils" for nothing. Moreover if she had asked five times as much I should have risen to the occasion, so odious would it have seemed to me to stand chaffering with Aspern's Juliana. It was queer enough to have a question of money with her at all. I assured her that her views perfectly met my own and that on the morrow I should have the pleasure of putting three months' rent into her hand. She received this announcement with apparent complacency and with no discoverable sense that after all it would become her to say that I ought to see the rooms first. This didn't occur to her, and indeed her serenity was mainly what I wanted. Our little agreement was just concluded when the door opened and the younger lady appeared on the threshold. As soon as Miss Bordereau saw her niece she cried out almost gaily: "He'll give three thousand—three thousand to-morrow!"

Miss Tina stood still, her patient eyes turning from one of us to the other; then she brought out, scarcely above her breath: "Do you mean francs?"

"Did you mean francs or dollars?" the old woman asked of me at this.

"I think francs were what you said," I sturdily smiled.

"That's very good," said Miss Tina, as if she had felt how over-reaching her own question might have looked.

"What do *you* know? You're ignorant," Miss Bordereau remarked; not with acerbity but with a strange soft coldness.

"Yes, of money—certainly of money!" Miss Tina hastened to concede.

"I'm sure you've your own fine branches of knowledge," I took the liberty of saying genially. There was something painful to me, somehow, in the turn the conversation had taken, in the discussion of dollars and francs.

"She had a very good education when she was young. I looked into that myself," said Miss Bordereau. Then she added: "But she has learned nothing since."

"I have always been with *you*," Miss Tina rejoined very mildly, and of a certainty with no intention of an epigram.

"Yes, but for that——!" her aunt declared with more satirical force. She evidently meant that but for this her niece would never have got on at all; the point of the observation, however, being lost on Miss Tina, though she blushed at hearing her history revealed to a stranger. Miss Bordereau went on, addressing herself to me: "And what time will you come to-morrow with the money?"

"The sooner the better. If it suits you I'll come at noon."

"I am always here, but I have my hours," said the old woman as if her convenience were not to be taken for granted.

"You mean the times when you receive?"

"I never receive. But I'll see you at noon, when you come with the money."

"Very good, I shall be punctual." To which I added: "May I

shake hands with you on our contract?" I thought there ought to be some little form; it would make me really feel easier, for I was sure there would be no other. Besides, though Miss Bordereau couldn't to-day be called personally attractive and there was something even in her wasted antiquity that bade one stand at one's distance, I felt an irresistible desire to hold in my own for a moment the hand Jeffrey Aspern had pressed.

For a minute she made no answer, and I saw that my proposal failed to meet with her approbation. She indulged in no movement of withdrawal, which I half-expected; she only said coldly: "I belong to a time when that was not the custom."

I felt rather snubbed but I exclaimed good-humouredly to Miss Tina, "Oh, you'll do as well!" I shook hands with her while she assented with a small flutter. "Yes, yes, to show it's all arranged!"

"Shall you bring the money in gold?" Miss Bordereau demanded as I was turning to the door.

I looked at her a moment. "Aren't you a little afraid, after all, of keeping such a sum as that in the house?" It was not that I was annoyed at her avidity, but was truly struck with the disparity between such a treasure and such scanty means of guarding it.

"Whom should I be afraid of if I'm not afraid of you?" she asked with her shrunken grimness.

"Ah, well," I laughed, "I shall be in point of fact a protector and I'll bring gold if you prefer."

"Thank you," the old woman returned with dignity and with an inclination of her head which evidently signified my dismissal. I passed out of the room, thinking how hard it would be to circumvent her. As I stood in the *sala* again I saw that Miss Tina had followed me, and I supposed that as her aunt had neglected to suggest I should take a look at my quarters it was her purpose to repair the omission. But she made no such overture; she only stood there with a dim, though not a languid smile, and with an effect of irresponsible incompetent youth almost comically at variance with the faded facts of her person. She was not infirm, like her aunt, but she struck me as more deeply futile, because her inefficiency was inward, which was not the case with Miss Bordereau's. I waited to see if she would offer to show me the rest of the house, but I didn't precipitate the question, inasmuch as my plan was from this moment to spend as much of my time as possible in her society. A minute indeed elapsed before I committed myself.

"I've had better fortune than I hoped. It was very kind of her to see me. Perhaps you said a good word for me."

"It was the idea of the money," said Miss Tina.

"And did you suggest that?"

"I told her you'd perhaps pay largely."

"What made you think that?"

"I told her I thought you were rich."

"And what put that into your head?"

"I don't know; the way you talked."

"Dear me, I must talk differently now," I returned. "I'm sorry to say it's not the case."

"Well," said Miss Tina, "I think that in Venice the *forestieri* in general often give a great deal for something that after all isn't much." She appeared to make this remark with a comforting intention, to wish to remind me that if I had been extravagant I wasn't foolishly singular. We walked together along the *sala*, and as I took its magnificent measure I said that I was afraid it wouldn't form a part of my *quartiere*. Were my rooms by chance to be among those that opened into it? "Not if you go above—to the second floor," she answered as if she had rather taken for granted I would know my proper place.

"And I infer that that's where your aunt would like me to be."

"She said your apartments ought to be very distinct."

"That certainly would be best." And I listened with respect while she told me that above I should be free to take whatever I might like; that there was another staircase, but only from the floor on which we stood, and that to pass from it to the garden-level or to come up to my lodging I should have in effect to cross the great hall. This was an immense point gained; I foresaw that it would constitute my whole leverage in my relations with the two ladies. When I asked Miss Tina how I was to manage at present to find my way up she replied with an access of that sociable shyness which constantly marked her manner:

"Perhaps you can't. I don't see—unless I should go with you."

She evidently hadn't thought of this before.

We ascended to the upper floor and visited a long succession of empty rooms. The best of them looked over the garden; some of the others had above the opposite rough-tiled house-tops a view of the blue lagoon. They were all dusty and even a little disfigured with long neglect, but I saw that by spending a few hundred francs I should be able to make three or four of them habitable enough. My experiment was turning out costly, yet now that I had all but taken possession I ceased to allow this to trouble me. I mentioned to my companion a few of the things I should put in, but she replied rather more precipitately than usual that I might do exactly what I liked: she seemed to wish to notify me that the Misses Bordereau would take none but the most veiled interest in my proceedings. I guessed that her aunt had instructed her to adopt this tone, and I may as well say now that I came afterwards to distinguish perfectly (as I believed) between the speeches she made on her own responsibility and those the old woman imposed upon her. She took no notice of the unswept condition of the rooms and indulged neither in explanations nor in apologies. I said to myself that this was a sign Juliana and her niece—disenchanting idea!— were untidy persons with a low Italian standard; but I afterwards recognised that a lodger who had forced an entrance had no *locus standi* as a critic. We looked out of a good many windows, for there was nothing within the rooms to look at, and still I wanted to linger. I asked her what several different objects in the prospect might be, but in no case did she appear to know. She was evidently not familiar with the view—it was as if she had not looked at it for years—and I presently saw that she was too preoccupied with something else to pretend to care for it. Suddenly she said—the remark was not suggested:

"I don't know whether it will make any difference to you, but the money is for me."

"The money——?"

"The money you're going to bring."

"Why, you'll make me wish to stay here two or three years!" I spoke as benevolently as possible, though it had begun to act on my nerves that these women so associated with Aspern should so constantly bring the pecuniary question back.

"That would be very good for me," she answered almost gaily. "You put me on my honour!"

She looked as if she failed to understand this, but went on: "She wants me to have more. She thinks she's going to die."

"Ah, not soon I hope!" I cried with genuine feeling. I had perfectly considered the possibility of her destroying her documents on the day she should feel her end at hand. I believed that she would cling to them till then, and I was as convinced of her reading Aspern's letters over every night or at least pressing them to her withered lips. I would have given a good deal for some view of those solemnities. I asked Miss Tina if her venerable relative were seriously ill, and she replied that she was only very tired—she had lived so extraordinarily long. That was what she said herself—she wanted to die for a change. Besides, all her friends had been dead for ages; either they ought to have remained or she ought to have gone. That was another thing her aunt often said: she was not at all resigned—resigned, that is, to life.

"But people don't die when they like, do they?" Miss Tina inquired. I took the liberty of asking why, if there was actually enough money to maintain both of them, there would not be more than enough in case of her being left alone. She considered this difficult problem a moment and then said: "Oh, well, you know, she takes care of me. She thinks that when I'm alone I shall be a great fool and shan't know how to manage."

"I should have supposed rather that you took care of *her*. I'm afraid she's very proud."

"Why, have you discovered that already?" Miss Tina cried with a dimness of glad surprise.

"I was shut up with her there for a considerable time and she struck me, she interested me extremely. It didn't take me long to make my discovery. She won't have much to say to me while I'm here."

"No, I don't think she will," my companion averred.

"Do you suppose she has some suspicion of me?"

Miss Tina's honest eyes gave me no sign I had touched a mark. "I shouldn't think so—letting you in after all so easily."

"You call it easily? She has covered her risk," I said. "But where is it one could take an advantage of her?"

"I oughtn't to tell you if I knew, ought I?" And Miss Tina added, before I had time to reply to this, smiling dolefully: "Do you think we've any weak points?"

"That's exactly what I'm asking. You'd only have to mention them for me to respect them religiously."

She looked at me hereupon with that air of timid but candid and even gratified curiosity with which she had confronted me from the first; after which she said: "There's nothing to tell. We're terribly quiet. I don't know how the days pass. We've no life."

"I wish I might think I should bring you a little."

"Oh, we know what we want," she went on. "It's all right."

There were twenty things I desired to ask her: how in the world they did live; whether they had any friends or visitors, any relations in America or in other countries. But I judged such probings premature; I must leave it to a later chance. "Well, don't *you* be proud," I contented myself with saying. "Don't hide from me altogether."

"Oh, I must stay with my aunt," she returned without looking at me. And at the same moment, abruptly, without any ceremony of parting, she quitted me and disappeared, leaving me to make my own way downstairs. I stayed a while longer, wandering about the bright desert—the sun was pouring in—of the old house, thinking the situation over on the spot. Not even the pattering little *serva* came to look after me, and I reflected that after all this treatment showed confidence.

IV

PERHAPS it did, but all the same, six weeks later, towards the middle of June, the moment when Mrs. Prest undertook her annual migration, I had made no measurable advance. I was obliged to confess to her that I had no results to speak of. My first step had been unexpectedly rapid, but there was no appearance it would be followed by a second. I was a thousand miles from taking tea with my hostesses—that privilege of which, as I reminded my good friend, we both had had a vision. She reproached me with lacking boldness and I answered that even to be bold you must have an opportunity: you may push on through a breach, but you can't batter down a dead wall. She returned that the breach I had already made was big enough to admit an army, and accused me of wasting precious hours in whimpering in her *salon* when I ought to have been carrying on the struggle in the field. It is true that I went to see her very often—all on the theory that it would console me (I freely expressed my discouragement) for my want of success on my own premises. But I began to feel that it didn't console me to be perpetually chaffed for my scruples, especially since I was really so vigilant; and I was rather glad when my ironic friend closed her house for the summer. She had expected to draw amusement from the drama of my intercourse with the Misses Bordereau, and was disappointed that the intercourse, and consequently the drama, had not come off. "They'll lead you on to your ruin," she said before she left Venice. "They'll get all your money without showing you a scrap." I think I settled down to my business with more concentration after her departure.

It was a fact that up to that time I had not, save on a single brief occasion, had even a moment's contact with my queer hostesses. The exception had occurred when I carried them according to my promise the terrible three thousand francs. Then I found Miss Tina awaiting me in the hall, and she took the money from my hand with a promptitude that prevented my seeing her aunt. The old lady had promised to receive me, yet apparently thought nothing of breaking that vow. The money was contained in a bag of chamois leather, of respectable dimensions, which my banker had given me, and Miss Tina had to make a big fist to receive it. This she did with extreme solemnity, though I tried to treat the affair a little as a joke. It was in no jocular strain, yet it was with a clearness akin to a brightness that she inquired, weighing the money in her two palms: "Don't you think it's too much?" To which I replied that this would depend on the amount of pleasure

I should get for it. Hereupon she turned away from me quickly, as
she had done the day before, murmuring in a tone different from
any she had used hitherto: "Oh, pleasure, pleasure—there's no
pleasure in this house!"

After that, for a long time, I never saw her, and I wondered the
common chances of the day shouldn't have helped us to meet. It
could only be evident that she was immensely on her guard against
them; and in addition to this the house was so big that for each
other we were lost in it. I used to look out for her hopefully as I
crossed the *sala* in my comings and goings, but I was not rewarded
with a glimpse of the tail of her dress. It was as if she never peeped
out of her aunt's apartment. I used to wonder what she did there
week after week and year after year. I had never met so stiff a policy
of seclusion; it was more than keeping quiet—it was like hunted
creatures feigning death. The two ladies appeared to have no
visitors whatever and no sort of contact with the world. I judged at
least that people couldn't have come to the house and that Miss
Tina couldn't have gone out without my catching some view of it.
I did what I disliked myself for doing—considering it but as once
in a way: I questioned my servant about their habits and let him
infer that I should be interested in any information he might glean.
But he gleaned amazingly little for a knowing Venetian: it must be
added that where there is a perpetual fast there are very few
crumbs on the floor. His ability in other ways was sufficient, if not
quite all I had attributed to him on the occasion of my first interview with Miss Tina. He had helped my gondolier to bring me
round a boat-load of furniture; and when these articles had been
carried to the top of the palace and distributed according to our
associated wisdom he organised my household with such dignity
as answered to its being composed exclusively of himself. He made
me in short as comfortable as I could be with my indifferent
prospects. I should have been glad if he had fallen in love with
Miss Bordereau's maid or, failing this, had taken her in aversion:
either event might have brought about some catastrophe, and a
catastrophe might have led to some parley. It was my idea that she
would have been sociable, and I myself on various occasions saw
her flit to and fro on domestic errands, so that I was sure she

was accessible. But I tasted of no gossip from that fountain, and I afterwards learned that Pasquale's affections were fixed upon an object that made him heedless of other women. This was a young lady with a powdered face, a yellow cotton gown and much leisure, who used often to come to see him. She practised, at her convenience, the art of a stringer of beads—these ornaments are made in Venice to profusion; she had her pocket full of them and I used to find them on the floor of my apartment—and kept an eye on the possible rival in the house. It was not for me of course to make the domestics tattle, and I never said a word to Miss Bordereau's cook.

It struck me as a proof of the old woman's resolve to have nothing to do with me that she should never have sent me a receipt for my three months' rent. For some days I looked out for it and then, when I had given it up, wasted a good deal of time in wondering what her reason had been for neglecting so indispensable and familiar a form. At first I was tempted to send her a reminder; after which I put by the idea—against my judgment as to what was right in the particular case—on the general ground of wishing to keep quiet. If Miss Bordereau suspected me of ulterior aims she would suspect me less if I should be businesslike, and yet I consented not to be. It was possible she intended her omission as an impertinence, a visible irony, to show how she could overreach people who attempted to overreach her. On that hypothesis it was well to let her see that one didn't notice her little tricks. The real reading of the matter, I afterwards gathered, was simply the poor lady's desire to emphasise the fact that I was in the enjoyment of a favour as rigidly limited as it had been liberally bestowed. She had given me part of her house, but she wouldn't add to that so much as a morsel of paper with her name on it. Let me say that even at first this didn't make me too miserable, for the whole situation had the charm of its oddity. I foresaw that I should have a summer after my own literary heart, and the sense of playing with my opportunity was much greater after all than any sense of being played with. There could be no Venetian business without patience, and since I adored the place I was much more in the spirit of it for having laid in a large provision. That spirit kept me perpetual company and seemed to look out at me from the revived immortal face—in which all his genius shone—of the great poet who was my prompter. I had invoked him and he had come; he hovered before me half the time; it was as if his bright ghost had returned to earth to assure me he regarded the affair as his own no less than as mine and that we should see it fraternally and fondly to a conclusion. It was as if he had said: "Poor dear, be easy with her; she has some natural prejudices; only give her time. Strange as it may appear to you she was very attractive in 1820. Meanwhile, aren't we in Venice together, and what better place is there for the meeting of dear friends? See how it glows with the advancing summer; how the sky and the sea and the rosy air and the marble of the palaces all shimmer and melt together." My eccentric private errand became a part of the general romance and the general glory—I felt even a mystic companionship, a moral fraternity with all those who in the past had been in the service of art. They had worked for beauty, for a devotion; and what else was I doing? That element was in every-thing that Jeffrey Aspern had written, and I was only bringing it to light.

I lingered in the *sala* when I went to and fro; I used to watch—as long as I thought decent—the door that led to Miss Bordereau's part of the house. A person observing me might have supposed I was trying to cast a spell on it or attempting some odd experiment in hypnotism. But I was only praying it might open or thinking what treasure probably lurked behind it. I hold it singular, as I look back, that I should never have doubted for a moment that the sacred relics were there; never have failed to know the joy of being beneath the same roof with them. After all they were under my hand—they had not escaped me yet—and they made my life continuous, in a fashion, with the illustrious life they had touched at the other end. I lost myself in this satisfaction to the point of assuming—in my quiet extravagance—that poor Miss Tina also went back, and still went back, as I used to phrase it. She did indeed, the gentle spinster, but not quite so far as Jeffrey Aspern, who was simply hearsay to her quite as he was to me. Only she had lived for years with Juliana, she had seen and handled all memen-toes and—even though she was stupid—some esoteric knowledge had rubbed off on her. That was what the old woman represented—esoteric knowledge; and this was the idea with which my critical heart used to thrill. It literally beat faster often of an evening when I had been out, as I stopped with my candle in the re-echoing hall on my way up to bed. It was as if at such a moment as that, in the stillness and after the long contradiction of the day, Miss Bordereau's secrets were in the air, the wonder of her survival more vivid. These were the acute impressions. I had them in another form, with more of a certain shade of reciprocity, during the hours I sat in the garden looking up over the top of my book at the closed windows of my hostess. In these windows no sign of life ever appeared; it was as if, for fear of my catching a glimpse of them, the two ladies passed their days in the dark. But this only emphasised their having matters to conceal; which was what I had wished to prove. Their motionless shutters became as expressive as eyes consciously closed, and I took comfort in the probability that, though invisible themselves, they kept me in view between the lashes.

I made a point of spending as much time as possible in the garden, to justify the picture I had originally given of my horticultural passion. And I not only spent time, but (hang it! as I said) spent precious money. As soon as I had got my rooms arranged and could give the question proper thought I surveyed the place with a clever expert and made terms for having it put in order. I was sorry to do this, for personally I liked it better as it was, with its weeds and its wild rich tangle, its sweet characteristic Venetian shabbiness. I had to be consistent, to keep my promise that I would smother the house in flowers. Moreover I clung to the fond fancy that by flowers I should make my way—I should succeed by big nosegays. I would batter the old women with lilies—I would bombard their citadel with roses. Their door would have to yield to the pressure when a mound of fragrance should be heaped against it. The place in truth had been brutally neglected. The Venetian capacity for dawdling is of the largest, and for a good many days unlimited litter was all my gardener had to show for his ministrations. There was a great digging of holes and carting about of earth, and after a while I grew so impatient that I had thoughts of sending for my "results" to the nearest stand. But I felt sure my

friends would see through the chinks of their shutters where such
tribute *couldn't* have been gathered, and might so make up their
minds against my veracity. I possessed my soul, and finally, though
the delay was long, perceived some appearances of bloom. This
encouraged me, and I waited serenely enough till they multiplied.
Meanwhile the real summer days arrived and began to pass, and as
I look back upon them they seem to me almost the happiest of my
life. I took more and more care to be in the garden whenever it was
not too hot. I had an arbour arranged and a low table and an
armchair put into it; and I carried out books and portfolios—I had
always some business of writing in hand—and worked and waited
and mused and hoped, while the golden hours elapsed and the
plants drank in the light and the inscrutable old palace turned pale
and then, as the day waned, began to recover and flush and my
papers rustled in the wandering breeze of the Adriatic.

Considering how little satisfaction I got from it at first it is
wonderful I shouldn't have grown more tired of trying to guess
what mystic rites of ennui the Misses Bordereau celebrated in their
darkened rooms; whether this had always been the tenor of their
life and how in previous years they had escaped elbowing their
neighbours. It was supposable they had then had other habits,
forms and resources; that they must once have been young or at
least middle-aged. There was no end to the questions it was
possible to ask about them and no end to the answers it was not
possible to frame. I had known many of my country-people in
Europe and was familiar with the strange ways they were liable to
take up there; but the Misses Bordereau formed altogether a new
type of the American absentee. Indeed it was clear the American
name had ceased to have any application to them—I had seen this
in the ten minutes I spent in the old woman's room. You could
never have said whence they came from the appearance of either of
them; wherever it was they had long ago shed and unlearned all
native marks and notes. There was nothing in them one recognised
or fitted, and, putting the question of speech aside, they might
have been Norwegians or Spaniards. Miss Bordereau, after all had
been in Europe nearly three-quarters of a century; it appeared by
some verses addressed to her by Aspern on the occasion of his own

second absence from America—verses of which Cumnor and I had after infinite conjecture established solidly enough the date—that she was even then, as a girl of twenty, on the foreign side of the sea. There was a profession in the poem—I hope not just for the phrase—that he had come back for her sake. We had no real light on her circumstances at that moment, any more than we had upon her origin, which we believed to be of the sort usually spoken of as modest. Cumnor had a theory that she had been a governess in some family in which the poet visited and that, in consequence of her position, there was from the first something unavowed, or rather something quite clandestine, in their relations. I on the other hand had hatched a little romance according to which she was the daughter of an artist, a painter or a sculptor, who had left the Western world, when the century was fresh, to study in the ancient schools. It was essential to my hypothesis that this amiable man should have lost his wife, should have been poor and unsuccessful and should have had a second daughter of a disposition quite different from Juliana's. It was also indispensable that he should have been accompanied to Europe by these young ladies and should have established himself there for the remainder of a struggling saddened life. There was a further implication that Miss Bordereau had had in her youth a perverse and reckless, albeit a generous and fascinating character, and that she had braved some wondrous chances. By what passions had she been ravaged, by what adventures and sufferings had she been blanched, what store of memories had she laid away for the monotonous future?

I asked myself these things as I sat spinning theories about her in my arbour and the bees droned in the flowers. It was incontestable that, whether for right or for wrong, most readers of certain of Aspern's poems (poems not as ambiguous as the sonnets—scarcely more divine, I think—of Shakespeare) had taken for granted that Juliana had not always adhered to the steep footway of renunciation. There hovered about her name a perfume of impenitent passion, an intimation that she had not been exactly as the respectable young person in general. Was this a sign that her singer had betrayed her, had given her away, as we say nowadays, to posterity? Certain it is that it would have been difficult to put one's

finger on the passage in which her fair fame suffered injury.
Moreover was not any fame fair enough that was so sure of dura-
tion and was associated with works immortal through their
beauty? It was a part of my idea that the young lady had had a
foreign lover—and say an unedifying tragical rupture—before her
meeting with Jeffrey Aspern. She had lived with her father and
sister in a queer old-fashioned expatriated artistic Bohemia of the
days when the esthetic was only the academic and the painters
who knew the best models for *contadina* and *pifferaro* wore peaked
hats and long hair. It was a society less awake than the coteries of
to-day—in its ignorance of the wonderful chances, the opportunities of the early bird, with which its path was strewn—to tatters of
old stuff and fragments of old crockery; so that Miss Bordereau
appeared not to have picked up or have inherited many objects of
importance. There was no enviable *bric-à-brac*, with its provoking
legend of cheapness, in the room in which I had seen her. Such a
fact as that suggested bareness, but none the less it worked happily
into the sentimental interest I had always taken in the early movements of my countrymen as visitors to Europe. When Americans
went abroad in 1820 there was something romantic, almost heroic
in it, as compared with the perpetual ferryings of the present hour,
the hour at which photography and other conveniences have anni-
hilated surprise. Miss Bordereau had sailed with her family on a
tossing brig in the days of long voyages and sharp differences; she
had had her emotions on the top of yellow diligences, passed the
night at inns where she dreamed of travellers' tales, and was
most struck, on reaching the Eternal City, with the elegance of
Roman pearls and scarfs and mosaic brooches. There was something touching to me in all that, and my imagination frequently
went back to the period. If Miss Bordereau carried it there of
course Jeffrey Aspern had at other times done so with greater
force. It was a much more important fact, if one was looking at his
genius critically, that he had lived in the days before the general
transfusion. It had happened to me to regret that he had known
Europe at all; I should have liked to see what he would have written
without that experience, by which he had incontestably been
enriched. But as his fate had ruled otherwise I went with him—I

tried to judge how the general old order would have struck him. It was not only there, however, I watched him; the relations he had entertained with the special new had even a livelier interest. His own country after all had had most of his life, and his muse, as they said at that time, was essentially American. That was originally what I had prized him for: that at a period when our native land was nude and crude and provincial, when the famous "atmosphere" it is supposed to lack was not even missed, when literature was lonely there and art and form almost impossible, he had found means to live and write like one of the first; to be free and general and not at all afraid; to feel, understand and express everything.

V

I WAS seldom at home in the evening, for when I attempted to occupy myself in my apartments the lamplight brought in a swarm of noxious insects, and it was too hot for closed windows. Accordingly I spent the late hours either on the water—the moonlights of Venice are famous—or in the splendid square which serves as a vast forecourt to the strange old church of Saint Mark. I sat in front of Florian's café eating ices, listening to music, talking with acquaintances: the traveller will remember how the immense cluster of tables and little chairs stretches like a promontory into the smooth lake of the Piazza. The whole place, of a summer's evening, under the stars and with all the lamps, all the voices and light footsteps on marble—the only sounds of the immense arcade that encloses it—is an open-air saloon dedicated to cooling drinks and to a still finer degustation, that of the splendid impressions received during the day. When I didn't prefer to keep mine to myself there was always a stray tourist, disencumbered of his Baedeker, to discuss them with, or some domesticated painter rejoicing in the return of the season of strong effects. The great basilica, with its low domes and bristling embroideries, the mystery of its mosaic and sculpture, looked ghostly in the tempered gloom, and the sea-breeze passed between the twin columns of the Piazzetta, the lintels of a door no longer guarded, as gently as if a rich curtain swayed there. I used sometimes on these occasions to think of the Misses Bordereau and of the pity of their being shut up in apartments which in the Venetian July even Venetian vastness couldn't relieve of some stuffiness. Their life seemed miles away from the life of the Piazza, and no doubt it was really too late to make the austere Juliana change her habits. But poor Miss Tina would have enjoyed one of Florian's ices, I was sure; sometimes I even had thoughts of carrying one home to her. Fortunately my patience bore fruit and I was not obliged to do anything so ridiculous.

One evening about the middle of July I came in earlier than usual—I forget what chance had led to this—and instead of going up to my quarters made my way into the garden. The temperature was very high; it was such a night as one would gladly have spent in the open air, and I was in no hurry to go to bed. I had floated home in my gondola, listening to the slow splash of the oar in the dark narrow canals, and now the only thought that occupied me was that it would be good to recline at one's length in the fragrant darkness on a garden-bench. The odour of the canal was doubtless at the bottom of that aspiration, and the breath of the garden, as I entered it, gave consistency to my purpose. It was delicious—just such an air as must have trembled with Romeo's vows when he stood among the thick flowers and raised his arms to his mistress's balcony. I looked at the windows of the palace to see if by chance the example of Verona—Verona being not far off—had been followed; but everything was dim, as usual, and everything was still. Juliana might on the summer nights of her youth have murmured down from open windows at Jeffrey Aspern, but Miss Tina was not a poet's mistress any more than I was a poet. This, however, didn't prevent my gratification from being great as I became aware on reaching the end of the garden that my younger *padrona* was seated in one of the bowers. At first I made out but an indistinct figure, not in the least counting on such an overture from one of my hostesses; it even occurred to me that some enamoured maid-servant had stolen in to keep a tryst with her sweetheart. I was going to turn away, not to frighten her, when the figure rose to its height and I recognised Miss Bordereau's niece. I must do myself the justice that I didn't wish to frighten her either, and much as I had longed for some such accident I should have been capable of retreating. It was as if I had laid a trap for her by coming home earlier than usual and by adding to that oddity my invasion of the garden. As she rose she spoke to me, and then I guessed that perhaps, secure in my almost inveterate absence, it was her nightly practice to take a lonely airing. There was no trap in truth, because I had had no suspicion. At first I took the words she uttered for an impatience of my arrival; but as she repeated them—I hadn't caught them clearly—I had the surprise of hearing her say: "Oh, dear, I'm so glad you've come!" She and her aunt had in common the property of unexpected speeches. She came out of the arbour almost as if to throw herself in my arms.

I hasten to add that I escaped this ordeal and that she didn't even shake hands with me. It was an ease to her to see me and presently she told me why—because she was nervous when out-of-doors at night alone. The plants and shrubs looked so strange in the dark, and there were all sorts of queer sounds—she couldn't tell me what they were—like the noises of animals. She stood close to me, looking about her with an air of greater security but without any demonstration of interest in me as an individual. Then I felt how little nocturnal prowlings could have been her habit, and I was also reminded—I had been afflicted by the same in talking with her before I took possession—that it was imposs-ible to allow too much for her simplicity.

"You speak as if you were lost in the backwoods," I cheeringly laughed. "How you manage to keep out of this charming place when you've only three steps to take to get into it is more than I've yet been able to discover. You hide away amazingly so long as I'm on the premises, I know; but I had a hope you peeped out a little at other times. You and your poor aunt are worse off than Carmelite nuns in their cells. Should you mind telling me how you exist without air, without exercise, without any sort of human contact? I don't see how you carry on the common business of life."

She looked at me as if I had spoken a strange tongue, and her answer was so little of one that I felt it make for irritation. "We go to bed very early—earlier than you'd believe." I was on the point of saying that this only deepened the mystery, but she gave me some relief by adding:

"Before you came we weren't so private. But I've never been out at night."

"Never in these fragrant alleys, blooming here under your nose?"

"Ah," said Miss Tina, "they were never nice till now!" There was a finer sense in this and a flattering comparison, so that it seemed to me I had gained some advantage. As I might follow that further by establishing a good grievance I asked her why, since she thought my garden nice, she had never thanked me in any way for the flowers I had been sending up in such quantities for the previous three weeks. I had not been discouraged—there had been, as she would have observed, a daily armful; but I had been brought up in the common forms and a word of recognition now and then would have touched me in the right place.

"Why, I didn't know they were for me!"

"They were for both of you. Why should I make a difference?"

Miss Tina reflected as if she might be thinking of a reason for that, but she failed to produce one. Instead of this she asked abruptly: "Why in the world do you want so much to know us?"

"I ought, after all, to make a difference," I replied. "That question's your aunt's; it isn't yours. You wouldn't ask it if you hadn't been put up to it."

"She didn't tell me to ask you," Miss Tina replied without confusion. She was, indeed, the oddest mixture of shyness and straightness.

"Well, she has often wondered about it herself and expressed her wonder to you. She has insisted on it, so that she has put the idea into your head that I'm insufferably pushing. Upon my word I think I've been very discreet. And how completely your aunt must have lost every tradition of sociability, to see anything out of the way in the idea that respectable intelligent people, living as we do under the same roof, should occasionally exchange a remark!

What could be more natural? We're of the same country and have at least some of the same tastes, since, like you, I'm intensely fond of Venice."

My friend seemed incapable of grasping more than one clause in any proposition, and she now spoke quickly, eagerly, as if she were answering my whole speech. "I'm not in the least fond of Venice. I should like to go far away!"

"Has she always kept you back so?" I went on, to show her I could be as irrelevant as herself.

"She told me to come out to-night; she has told me very often," said Miss Tina. "It is I who wouldn't come. I don't like to leave her."

"Is she too weak, is she really failing?" I demanded, with more emotion, I think, than I meant to betray. I measured this by the way her eyes rested on me in the darkness. It embarrassed me a little, and to turn the matter off I continued genially: "Do let us sit down together comfortably somewhere—while you tell me all about her."

Miss Tina made no resistance to this. We found a bench less secluded, less confidential, as it were, than the one in the arbour; and we were still sitting there when I heard midnight ring out from those clear bells of Venice which vibrate with a solemnity of their own over the lagoon and hold the air so much more than the chimes of other places. We were together more than an hour, and our interview gave, as it struck me, a great lift to my undertaking. Miss Tina accepted the situation without a protest; she had avoided me for three months, yet now she treated me almost as if these three months had made me an old friend. If I had chosen I might have gathered from this that though she had avoided me she had given a good deal of consideration to doing so. She paid no attention to the flight of time—never worried at my keeping her so long away from her aunt. She talked freely, answering questions and asking them and not even taking advantage of certain longish pauses by which they were naturally broken to say she thought she had better go in. It was almost as if she were waiting for some-thing—something I might say to her—and intended to give me my opportunity. I was the more struck by this as she told me how much less well her aunt had been for a good many days, and in a way that was rather new. She was markedly weaker; at moments she showed no strength at all; yet more than ever before she wished to be left alone. That was why she had told her to come out—not even to remain in her own room, which was alongside; she pronounced poor Miss Tina "a worry, a bore and a source of aggravation." She sat still for hours together, as if for long sleep; she had always done that, musing and dozing; but at such times formerly she gave, in breaks, some small sign of life, of interest, liking her companion to be near her with her work. This sad personage confided to me that at present her aunt was so motionless as to create the fear she was dead; moreover she scarce ate or drank—one couldn't see what she lived on. The great thing was that she still on most days got up; the serious job was to dress her, to wheel her out of her bedroom. She clung to as many of her old habits as possible and had always, little company as they had received for years, made a point of sitting in the great parlour.

I scarce knew what to think of all this—of Miss Tina's sudden conversion to sociability and of the strange fact that the more the old woman appeared to decline to her end the less she should desire to be looked after. The story hung indifferently together, and I even asked myself if it mightn't be a trap laid for me, the result of a design to make me show my hand. I couldn't have told why my companions (as they could only by courtesy be called) should have this purpose—why they should try to trip up so lucrative a lodger. But at any hazard I kept on my guard, so that Miss Tina shouldn't have occasion again to ask me what I might really be "up to." Poor woman, before we parted for the night my mind was at rest as to what *she* might be. She was up to nothing at all.

She told me more about their affairs than I had hoped; there was no need to be prying, for it evidently drew her out simply to feel me listen and care. She ceased wondering why I *should*, and at last, while describing the brilliant life they had led years before, she almost chattered. It was Miss Tina who judged it brilliant; she said that when they first came to live in Venice, years and years back— I found her essentially vague about dates and the order in which events had occurred—there was never a week they hadn't some visitor or didn't make some pleasant *passeggio* in the town. They had seen all the curiosities; they had even been to the Lido in a boat—she spoke as if I might think there was a way on foot; they had had a collation there, brought in three baskets and spread out on the grass. I asked her what people they had known and she said, Oh, very nice ones—the Cavaliere Bombicci and the Contessa Altemura, with whom they had had a great friendship! Also English people—the Churtons and the Goldies and Mrs. Stock-Stock, whom they had loved dearly; she was dead and gone, poor dear. That was the case with most of their kind circle—this expression was Miss Tina's own; though a few were left, which was a wonder considering how they had neglected them. She mentioned the names of two or three Venetian old women; of a certain doctor, very clever, who was so attentive—he came as a friend, he had really given up practice; of the *avvocato* Pochintesta, who wrote beautiful poems and had addressed one to her aunt. These people came to see them without fail every year, usually at the *capo d'anno*, and of old her aunt used to make them some little present—her aunt and she together: small things that she, Miss Tina, turned out with her own hand, paper lamp-shades, or mats for the decanters of wine at dinner, or those woollen things that in cold weather are worn on the wrists. The last few years there hadn't been many presents; she couldn't think what to make and her aunt had lost interest and never suggested. But the people came all the same; if the good Venetians liked you once they liked you for ever.

There was affecting matter enough in the good faith of this sketch of former social glories; the picnic at the Lido had remained vivid through the ages and poor Miss Tina evidently was of the impression that she had had a dashing youth. She had in fact had a glimpse of the Venetian world in its gossiping home-keeping parsimonious professional walks; for I noted for the first time how nearly she had acquired by contact the trick of the familiar soft-sounding almost infantile prattle of the place. I judged her to have imbibed this invertebrate dialect from the natural way the names of things and people—mostly purely local—rose to her lips. If she knew little of what they represented she knew still less of anything else. Her aunt had drawn in—the failure of interest in the table-mats and lamp-shades was a sign of that—and she hadn't been able to mingle in society or to entertain it alone; so that her range of reminiscence struck one as an old world altogether. Her tone, hadn't it been so decent, would have seemed to carry one back to the queer rococo Venice of Goldoni and Casanova. I found myself mistakenly think of her too as one of Jeffrey Aspern's contemporaries; this came from her having so little in common with my own. It was possible, I indeed reasoned, that she hadn't even heard of him; it might very well be that Juliana had forborne to lift for innocent eyes the veil that covered the temple of her glory. In this case she perhaps wouldn't know of the existence of the papers, and I welcomed that presumption—it made me feel more safe with her—till I remembered we had believed the letter of disavowal received by Cumnor to be in the handwriting of the niece. If it had been dictated to her she had of course to know what it was about; though the effect of it withal was to repudiate the idea of any connection with the poet. I held it probable at all events that Miss Tina hadn't read a word of his poetry. Moreover if, with her companion, she had always escaped invasion and research, there was little occasion for her having got it into her head that people were "after" the letters. People had not been after them, for people hadn't heard of them. Cumnor's fruitless feeler would have been a solitary accident.

When midnight sounded Miss Tina got up; but she stopped at the door of the house only after she had wandered two or three times with me round the garden. "When shall I see you again?" I asked before she went in; to which she replied with promptness that she should like to come out the next night. She added, however, that she shouldn't come—she was so far from doing everything she liked.

"You might do a few things *I* like," I quite sincerely sighed.

"Oh, you—I don't believe you!" she murmured at this, facing me with her simple solemnity.

"Why don't you believe me?"

"Because I don't understand you."

"That's just the sort of occasion to have faith." I couldn't say more, though I should have liked to, as I saw I only mystified her; for I had no wish to have it on my conscience that I might pass for having made love to her. Nothing less should I have seemed to do had I continued to beg a lady to "believe in me" in an Italian garden on a midsummer night. There was some merit in my scruples, for Miss Tina lingered and lingered: I made out in her the conviction that she shouldn't really soon come down again and the wish therefore to protract the present. She insisted, too, on making the talk between us personal to ourselves; and altogether her behaviour was such as would have been possible only to a perfectly artless and a considerably witless woman.

"I shall like the flowers better now that I know them also meant for me."

"How could you have doubted it? If you'll tell me the kind you like best I'll send a double lot."

"Oh, I like them all best!" Then she went on familiarly: "Shall you study—shall you read and write—when you go up to your rooms?"

"I don't do that at night—at this season. The lamplight brings in the animals."

"You might have known that when you came."

"I did know it!"

"And in winter do you work at night?"

"I read a good deal, but I don't often write." She listened as if these details had a rare interest, and suddenly a temptation quite at odds with all the prudence I had been teaching myself glimmered at me in her plain mild face. Ah, yes, she was safe and I could make her safer! It seemed to me from one moment to another that I couldn't wait longer—that I really must take a sounding. So I went on: "In general before I go to sleep (very often in bed; it's a bad habit, but I confess to it) I read some great poet. In nine cases out of ten it's a volume of Jeffrey Aspern."

I watched her well as I pronounced that name, but I saw nothing wonderful. Why should I indeed? Wasn't Jeffrey Aspern the property of the human race?

"Oh, we read him—we have read him," she quietly replied.

"He's my poet of poets—I know him almost by heart."

For an instant Miss Tina hesitated; then her sociability was too much for her. "Oh, by heart—that's nothing;" and, though dimly, she quite lighted. "My aunt used to know him, to know him"—she paused an instant and I wondered what she was going to say—"to know him as a visitor."

"As a visitor?" I guarded my tone.

"He used to call on her and take her out."

I continued to stare. "My dear lady, he died a hundred years ago!"

"Well," she said amusingly, "my aunt's a hundred and fifty."

"Mercy on us!" I cried; "why didn't you tell me before? I should like so to ask her about him."

"She wouldn't care for that—she wouldn't tell you," Miss Tina returned.

"I don't care what she cares for! She *must* tell me—it's not a chance to be lost."

"Oh, you should have come twenty years ago. Then she still talked about him."

"And what did she say?" I eagerly asked.

"I don't know—that he liked her immensely."

"And she—didn't she like *him*?"

"She said he was a god." Miss Tina gave me this information flatly, without expression; her tone might have made it a piece of trivial gossip. But it stirred me deeply as she dropped the words into the summer night; their sound might have been the light rustle of an old unfolded love-letter.

"Fancy, fancy!" I murmured. And then: "Tell me this, please— has she got a portrait of him? They're distressingly rare."

"A portrait? I don't know," said Miss Tina; and now there was discomfiture in her face. "Well, good-night!" she added; and she turned into the house.

I accompanied her into the wide dusky stone-paved passage that corresponded on the ground floor with our grand *sala*. It opened at one end into the garden, at the other upon the canal, and was lighted now only by the small lamp always left for me to take up as I went to bed. An extinguished candle which Miss Tina apparently had brought down with her stood on the same table with it. "Good-night, good-night!" I replied, keeping beside her as she went to get her light. "Surely you'd know, shouldn't you, if she had one?"

"If she had what?" the poor lady asked, looking at me queerly over the flame of her candle.

"A portrait of the god. I don't know what I wouldn't give to see it."

"I don't know what she has got. She keeps her things locked up." And Miss Tina went away toward the staircase with the sense evidently of having said too much.

I let her go—I wished not to frighten her—and I contented myself with remarking that Miss Bordereau wouldn't have locked up such a glorious possession as that: a thing a person would be proud of and hang up in a prominent place on the parlour-wall. Therefore of course she hadn't any portrait. Miss Tina made no direct answer to this and, candle in hand, with her back to me, mounted two or three degrees. Then she stopped short and turned round, looking at me across the dusky space.

"Do you write—do you write?" There was a shake in her voice—she could scarcely bring it out.

"Do I write? Oh, don't speak of my writing on the same day with Aspern's!"

"Do you write about *him*—do you pry into his life?"

"Ah, that's your aunt's question; it can't be yours!" I said, in a tone of slightly wounded sensibility.

"All the more reason then that you should answer it. Do you please?"

I thought I had allowed for the falsehoods I should have to tell, but I found that in fact when it came to the point I hadn't. Besides, now that I had an opening there was a kind of relief in being frank. Lastly—it was perhaps fanciful, even fatuous—I guessed that Miss Tina personally wouldn't in the last resort be less my friend. So after a moment's hesitation I answered: "Yes, I've written about him and I'm looking for more material. In heaven's name have you got any?"

"*Santo Dio!*" she exclaimed without heeding my question; and she hurried upstairs and out of sight. I might count upon her in the last resort, but for the present she was visibly alarmed. The proof of it was that she began to hide again, so that for a fortnight

I kept missing her. I found my patience ebbing, and after four or five days of this I told the gardener to stop the "floral tributes."

VI

ONE afternoon, at last, however, as I came down from my quarters to go out, I found her in the *sala*: it was our first encounter on that ground since I had come to the house. She put on no air of being there by accident; there was an ignorance of such arts in her honest angular diffidence. That I might be quite sure she was waiting for me she mentioned it at once, but telling me with it that Miss Bordereau wished to see me: she would take me into the room at that moment if I had time. If I had been late for a love-tryst I would have stayed for this, and I quickly signified that I should be delighted to wait on my benefactress. "She wants to talk with you—to know you," Miss Tina said, smiling as if she herself appreciated that idea; and she led me to the door of her aunt's apartment. I stopped her a moment before she had opened it, looking at her with some curiosity. I told her that this was a great satisfaction to me and a great honour; but all the same I should like to ask what had made Miss Bordereau so markedly and suddenly change. It had been only the other day that she wouldn't suffer me near her. Miss Tina was not embarrassed by my question; she had as many little unexpected serenities, plausibilities almost, as if she told fibs, but the odd part of them was that they had on the contrary their source in her truthfulness. "Oh, my aunt varies," she answered; "it's so terribly dull—I suppose she's tired."

"But you told me she wanted more and more to be alone."

Poor Miss Tina coloured as if she found me too pushing. "Well, if you don't believe she wants to see you, I haven't invented it! I think people often are capricious when they're very old."

"That's perfectly true. I only wanted to be clear as to whether you've repeated to her what I told you the other night."

"What you told me?"

"About Jeffrey Aspern—that I'm looking for materials."

"If I had told her do you think she'd have sent for you?"

"That's exactly what I want to know. If she wants to keep him to herself she might have sent for me to tell me so."

"She won't speak of him," said Miss Tina. Then as she opened the door she added in a lower tone: "I told her nothing."

The old woman was sitting in the same place in which I had seen her last, in the same position, with the same mystifying bandage over her eyes. Her welcome was to turn her almost invisible face to me and show me that while she sat silent she saw me clearly. I made no motion to shake hands with her; I now felt too well that this was out of place for ever. It had been sufficiently enjoined on me that she was too sacred for trivial modernisms— too venerable to touch. There was something so grim in her aspect—it was partly the accident of her green shade—as I stood there to be measured, that I ceased on the spot to doubt her suspecting me, though I didn't in the least myself suspect that Miss Tina hadn't just spoken the truth. She hadn't betrayed me, but the old woman's brooding instinct had served her; she had turned me over and over in the long still hours and had guessed. The worst of it was that she looked terribly like an old woman who at a pinch would, even like Sardanapalus, burn her treasure. Miss Tina pushed a chair forward, saying to me, "This will be a good place for you to sit." As I took possession of it I asked after Miss Bordereau's health; expressed the hope that in spite of the very hot weather it was satisfactory. She answered that it was good enough—good enough; that it was a great thing to be alive.

"Oh, as to that, it depends upon what you compare it with!" I returned with a laugh.

"I don't compare—I don't compare. If I did that I should have given everything up long ago."

I liked to take this for a subtle allusion to the rapture she had known in the society of Jeffrey Aspern—though it was true that such an allusion would have accorded ill with the wish I imputed to her to keep him buried in her soul. What it accorded with was my constant conviction that no human being had ever had a happier social gift than his, and what it seemed to convey was that nothing in the world was worth speaking of if one pretended to speak of that. But one didn't pretend! Miss Tina sat down beside her aunt, looking as if she had reason to believe some wonderful talk would come off between us.

"It's about the beautiful flowers," said the old lady; "you sent us so many—I ought to have thanked you for them before. But I don't write letters and I receive company but at long intervals."

She hadn't thanked me while the flowers continued to come, but she departed from her custom so far as to send for me as soon as she began to fear they wouldn't come any more. I noted this; I remembered what an acquisitive propensity she had shown when it was a question of extracting gold from me, and I privately rejoiced at the happy thought I had had in suspending my tribute. She had missed it and was willing to make a concession to bring it back. At the first sign of this concession I could only go to meet her. "I'm afraid you haven't had many, of late, but they shall begin again immediately—to-morrow, to-night."

"Oh, do send us some to-night!" Miss Tina cried as if it were a great affair.

"What else should you do with them? It isn't a manly taste to make a bower of your room," the old woman remarked.

"I don't make a bower of my room, but I'm exceedingly fond of growing flowers, of watching their ways. There's nothing unmanly in that; it has been the amusement of philosophers, of statesmen in retirement; even, I think, of great captains."

"I suppose you know you can sell them—those you don't use," Miss Bordereau went on. "I daresay they wouldn't give you much for them; still, you could make a bargain."

"Oh, I've never in my life made a bargain, as you ought pretty well to have gathered. My gardener disposes of them and I ask no questions."

"I'd ask a few, I can promise you!" said Miss Bordereau; and it was so I first heard the strange sound of her laugh, which was as if the faint "walking" ghost of her old-time tone had suddenly cut a caper. I couldn't get used to the idea that this vision of pecuniary profit was most what drew out the divine Juliana.

"Come into the garden yourself and pick them; come as often

as you like; come every day. The flowers are all for you," I pursued, addressing Miss Tina and carrying off this veracious statement by treating it as an innocent joke. "I can't imagine why she doesn't come down," I added for Miss Bordereau's benefit.

"You must make her come; you must come up and fetch her," the old woman said to my stupefaction. "That odd thing you've made in the corner will do very well for her to sit in."

The allusion to the most elaborate of my shady coverts, a sketchy "summer-house," was irreverent; it confirmed the impression I had already received that there was a flicker of impertinence in Miss Bordereau's talk, a vague echo of the boldness or the archness of her adventurous youth and which had somehow automatically outlived passions and faculties. None the less I asked: "Wouldn't it be possible for you to come down there yourself? Wouldn't it do you good to sit there in the shade and the sweet air?"

"Oh, sir, when I move out of this it won't be to sit in the air, and I'm afraid that any that may be stirring around me won't be particularly sweet! It will be a very dark shade indeed. But that won't be just yet," Miss Bordereau continued cannily, as if to correct any hopes this free glance at the last receptacle of her mortality might lead me to entertain. "I've sat here many a day and have had enough of arbours in my time. But I'm not afraid to wait till I'm called."

Miss Tina had expected, as I felt, rare conversation, but perhaps she found it less gracious on her aunt's side—considering I had been sent for with a civil intention—than she had hoped. As to give the position a turn that would put our companion in a light more favourable she said to me: "Didn't I tell you the other night that she had sent me out? You see I can do what I like!"

"Do you pity her—do you teach her to pity herself?" Miss Bordereau demanded, before I had time to answer this appeal. "She has a much easier life than I had at her age."

"You must remember it has been quite open to me," I said, "to think you rather inhuman."

"Inhuman? That's what the poets used to call the women a hundred years ago. Don't try that; you won't do as well as they!"

Juliana went on. "There's no more poetry in the world—that *I* know of at least. But I won't bandy words with you," she said, and I well remember the old-fashioned artificial sound she gave the speech. "You make me talk, talk, talk! It isn't good for me at all." I got up at this and told her I would take no more of her time; but she detained me to put a question. "Do you remember, the day I saw you about the rooms, that you offered us the use of your gondola?" And when I assented promptly, struck again with her disposition to make a "good thing" of my being there and wondering what she now had in her eye, she produced: "Why don't you take that girl out in it and show her the place?"

"Oh, dear aunt, what do you want to do with me?" cried the "girl" with a piteous quaver. "I know all about the place!"

"Well, then, go with him and explain!" said Miss Bordereau, who gave an effect of cruelty to her implacable power of retort. This showed her as a sarcastic profane cynical old woman. "Haven't we heard that there have been all sorts of changes in all these years? You ought to see them, and at your age—I don't mean because you're so young—you ought to take the chances that come. You're old enough, my dear, and this gentleman won't hurt you. He'll show you the famous sunsets, if they still go on—*do* they go on? The sun set for me so long ago. But that's not a reason. Besides, I shall never miss you; you think you're too important. Take her to the Piazza; it used to be very pretty," Miss Bordereau continued, addressing herself to me. "What have they done with the funny old church? I hope it hasn't tumbled down. Let her look at the shops; she may take some money, she may buy what she likes."

Poor Miss Tina had got up, discountenanced and helpless, and as we stood there before her aunt it would certainly have struck a spectator of the scene that our venerable friend was making rare sport of us. Miss Tina protested in a confusion of exclamations and murmurs; but I lost no time in saying that if she would do me the honour to accept the hospitality of my boat I would engage she really shouldn't be bored. Or if she didn't want so much of my company the boat itself, with the gondolier, was at her service; he was a capital oar and she might have every confidence. Miss Tina, without definitely answering this speech, looked away from me and out of the window, quite as if about to weep, and I remarked that once we had Miss Bordereau's approval we could easily come to an understanding. We would take an hour, whichever she liked, one of the very next days. As I made my obeisance to the old lady I asked her if she would kindly permit me to see her again.

For a moment she kept me; then she said: "Is it very necessary to your happiness?"

"It diverts me more than I can say."

"You're wonderfully civil. Don't you know it almost kills *me*?"

"How can I believe that when I see you more animated, more brilliant than when I came in?"

"That's very true, aunt," said Miss Tina. "I think it does you good."

"Isn't it touching, the solicitude we each have that the other shall enjoy herself?" sneered Miss Bordereau. "If you think me brilliant to-day you don't know what you're talking about; you've never seen an agreeable woman. What do you people know about good society?" she cried; but before I could tell her, "Don't try to pay me a compliment; I've been spoiled," she went on. "My door's shut, but you may sometimes knock."

With this she dismissed me and I left the room. The latch closed behind me, but Miss Tina, contrary to my hope, had remained within. I passed slowly across the hall and before taking my way downstairs waited a little. My hope was answered; after a minute my conductress followed me. "That's a delightful idea about the Piazza," I said. "When will you go—to-night, to-morrow?"

She had been disconcerted, as I have mentioned, but I had already perceived, and I was to observe again, that when Miss Tina was embarrassed she didn't—as most women would have in like case—turn away, floundering and hedging, but came closer, as it were, with a deprecating, a clinging appeal to be spared, to be protected. Her attitude was a constant prayer for aid and explanation, and yet no woman in the world could have been less of a comedian. From the moment you were kind to her she depended on you absolutely; her self-consciousness dropped and she took the greatest intimacy, the innocent intimacy that was all she could conceive, for granted. She didn't know, she now declared, what possessed her aunt, who had changed so quickly, who had got some idea. I replied that she must catch the idea and let me have it: we would go and take an ice together at Florian's and she should report while we listened to the band.

"Oh, it will take me a long time to be able to 'report'!" she said rather ruefully; and she could promise me this satisfaction neither for that night nor for the next. I was patient now, however, for I felt I had only to wait; and in fact at the end of the week, one lovely evening after dinner, she stepped into my gondola, to which in honour of the occasion I had attached a second oar.

We swept in the course of five minutes into the Grand Canal; whereupon she uttered a murmur of ecstasy as fresh as if she had been a tourist just arrived. She had forgotten the splendour of the great water-way on a clear summer evening, and how the sense of floating between marble palaces and reflected lights disposed the mind to freedom and ease. We floated long and far, and though my friend gave no high-pitched voice to her glee I was sure of her full surrender. She was more than pleased, she was transported; the whole thing was an immense liberation. The gondola moved with slow strokes, to give her time to enjoy it, and she listened to the splash of the oars, which grew louder and more musically liquid as we passed into narrow canals, as if it were a revelation of Venice. When I asked her how long it was since she had thus floated she answered: "Oh, I don't know; a long time—not since my aunt began to be ill." This was not the only show of her extreme vagueness about the previous years and the line marking off the period of Miss Bordereau's eminence. I was not at liberty to keep her out long, but we took a considerable *giro* before going to the Piazza. I asked her no questions, holding off by design from her life at home and the things I wanted to know; I poured, rather, treasures of information about the objects before and around us into her ears, describing also Florence and Rome, discoursing on the charms and advantages of travel. She reclined, receptive, on the deep leather cushions, turned her eyes conscientiously to everything I noted and never mentioned to me till some time afterwards that she might be supposed to know Florence better than I, as she had lived there for years with her kinswoman. At last she said with the shy impatience of a child: "Are we not really going to the Piazza? That's what I want to see!" I immediately gave the order that we should go straight, after which we sat silent with the expectation of arrival. As some time still passed, however, she broke out of her own movement: "I've found out what's the matter with my aunt: she's afraid you'll go!"

I quite gasped. "What has put that into her head?"

"She has had an idea you've not been happy. That's why she's different now."

"You mean, she wants to make me happier?"

"Well, she wants you not to go. She wants you to stay."

"I suppose you mean on account of the rent," I remarked candidly.

Miss Tina's candour but profited. "Yes, you know; so that I shall have more."

"How much does she want you to have?" I asked with all the gaiety I now felt. "She ought to fix the sum, so that I may stay till it's made up."

"Oh, that wouldn't please me," said Miss Tina. "It would be unheard of, your taking that trouble."

"But suppose I should have my own reasons for staying in Venice?"

"Then it would be better for you to stay in some other house."

"And what would your aunt say to that?"

"She wouldn't like it at all. But I should think you'd do well to give up your reasons and go away altogether."

"Dear Miss Tina," I said, "it's not so easy to give up my reasons!"

She made no immediate answer to this, but after a moment broke out afresh: "I think I know what your reasons are!"

"I daresay, because the other night I almost told you how I wished you'd help me to make them good."

"I can't do that without being false to my aunt."

"What do you mean by being false to her?"

"Why, she would never consent to what you want. She has been asked, she has been written to. It makes her fearfully angry."

"Then she *has* papers of value?" I precipitately cried.

"Oh, she has everything!" sighed Miss Tina with a curious weariness, a sudden lapse into gloom.

These words caused all my pulses to throb, for I regarded them as precious evidence. I felt them too deeply to speak, and in the interval the gondola approached the Piazzetta. After we had disembarked I asked my companion if she would rather walk round the square or go and sit before the great café; to which she replied that she would do whichever I liked best—I must only remember again how little time she had. I assured her there was plenty to do both, and we made the circuit of the long arcades. Her spirits revived at the sight of the bright shop-windows, and she lingered and stopped, admiring or disapproving of their contents, asking me what I thought of things, theorising about prices. My attention wandered from her; her words of a while before, "Oh, she has everything!" echoed so in my consciousness. We sat down at last in the crowded circle at Florian's, finding an unoccupied table among those that were ranged in the square. It was a splendid night and all the world out-of-doors; Miss Tina couldn't have wished the elements more auspicious for her return to society. I saw she felt it all even more than she told, but her impressions were well-nigh too many for her. She had forgotten the attraction of the world and was learning that she had for the best years of her life been rather mercilessly cheated of it. This didn't make her angry; but as she took in the charming scene her face had, in spite of its smile of appreciation, the flush of a wounded surprise. She didn't speak, sunk in the sense of opportunities, for ever lost, that ought to have been easy; and this gave me a chance to say to her: "Did you mean a while ago that your aunt has a plan of keeping me on by admitting me occasionally to her presence?"

"She thinks it will make a difference with you if you sometimes see her. She wants you so much to stay that she's willing to make that concession."

"And what good does she consider I think it will do me to see her?"

"I don't know; it must be interesting," said Miss Tina simply.

"You told her you found it so."

"So I did; but every one doesn't think that."

"No, of course not, or more people would try."

"Well, if she's capable of making that reflexion she's capable also of making this further one," I went on: "that I must have a particular reason for not doing as others do, in spite of the interest she offers—for not leaving her alone." Miss Tina looked as if she failed to grasp this rather complicated proposition; so I continued: "If you've not told her what I said to you the other night may she not at least have guessed it?"

"I don't know—she's very suspicious."

"But she hasn't been made so by indiscreet curiosity, by persecution?"

"No, no; it isn't that," said Miss Tina, turning on me a troubled face. "I don't know how to say it: it's on account of something—ages ago, before I was born—in her life."

"Something? What sort of thing?"—and I asked it as if I could have no idea.

"Oh, she has never told me." And I was sure my friend spoke the truth.

Her extreme limpidity was almost provoking, and I felt for the moment that she would have been more satisfactory if she had been less ingenuous. "Do you suppose it's something to which Jeffrey Aspern's letters and papers—I mean the things in her possession—have reference?"

"I daresay it is!" my companion exclaimed as if this were a very happy suggestion. "I've never looked at any of those things."

"None of them? Then how do you know what they are?"

"I don't," said Miss Tina placidly. "I've never had them in my hands. But I've seen them when she has had them out."

"Does she have them out often?"

"Not now, but she used to. She's very fond of them."

"In spite of their being compromising?"

"Compromising?" Miss Tina repeated as if vague as to what that meant. I felt almost as one who corrupts the innocence of youth.

"I allude to their containing painful memories."

"Oh, I don't think anything's painful."

"You mean there's nothing to affect her reputation?"

An odder look even than usual came at this into the face of Miss Bordereau's niece—a confession, it seemed, of helplessness, an appeal to me to deal fairly, generously with her. I had brought her to the Piazza, placed her among charming influences, paid her an attention she appreciated, and now I appeared to show it all as a bribe—a bribe to make her turn in some way against her aunt. She was of a yielding nature and capable of doing almost anything to please a person markedly kind to her; but the greatest kindness of all would be not to presume too much on this. It was strange enough, as I afterwards thought, that she had not the least air of resenting my want of consideration for her aunt's character, which would have been in the worst possible taste if anything less vital—from my point of view—had been at stake. I don't think she really measured it. "Do you mean she ever did something bad?" she asked in a moment.

"Heaven forbid I should say so, and it's none of my business. Besides, if she did," I agreeably put it, "that was in other ages, in another world. But why shouldn't she destroy her papers?"

"Oh, she loves them too much."

"Even now, when she may be near her end?"

"Perhaps when she's sure of that she will."

"Well, Miss Tina," I said, "that's just what I should like you to prevent."

"How can I prevent it?"

"Couldn't you get them away from her?"

"And give them to you?"

This put the case, superficially, with sharp irony, but I was sure of her not intending that. "Oh, I mean that you might let me see them and look them over. It isn't for myself, or that I should want them at any cost to any one else. It's simply that they would be of such immense interest to the public, such immeasurable importance as a contribution to Jeffrey Aspern's history."

She listened to me in her usual way, as if I abounded in matters she had never heard of, and I felt almost as base as the reporter of a newspaper who forces his way into a house of mourning. This was marked when she presently said: "There was a gentleman who some time ago wrote to her in very much those words. He also wanted her papers."

"And did she answer him?" I asked, rather ashamed of not having my friend's rectitude.

"Only when he had written two or three times. He made her very angry."

"And what did she say?"

"She said he was a devil," Miss Tina replied categorically.

"She used that expression in her letter?"

"Oh, no; she said it to me. She made me write to him."

"And what did you say?"

"I told him there were no papers at all."

"Ah, poor gentleman!" I groaned.

"I knew there were, but I wrote what she bade me."

"Of course you had to do that. But I hope I shan't pass for a devil."

"It will depend upon what you ask me to do for you," my companion smiled.

"Oh, if there's a chance of *your* thinking so my affair's in a bad way! I shan't ask you to steal for me, nor even to fib—for you *can't* fib, unless on paper. But the principal thing is this—to prevent her destroying the papers."

"Why, I've no control of her," said Miss Tina. "It's she who controls me."

"But she doesn't control her own arms and legs, does she? The way she would naturally destroy her letters would be to burn them. Now she can't burn them without fire, and she can't get fire unless you give it her."

"I've always done everything she has asked," my poor friend pleaded. "Besides, there's Olimpia."

I was on the point of saying that Olimpia was probably corruptible, but I thought it best not to sound that note. So I simply put it that this frail creature might perhaps be managed.

"Every one can be managed by my aunt," said Miss Tina. And then she remembered that her holiday was over; she must go home.

I laid my hand on her arm, across the table, to stay her a moment. "What I want of you is a general promise to help me."

"Oh, how *can* I, how *can* I?" she asked, wondering and troubled. She was half-surprised, half-frightened at my attaching that importance to her, at my calling on her for action.

"This is the main thing: to watch our friend carefully and warn me in time, before she commits that dreadful sacrilege."

"I can't watch her when she makes me go out."

"That's very true."

"And when you do too."

"Mercy on us—do you think she'll have done anything to-night?"

"I don't know. She's very cunning."

"Are you trying to frighten me?" I asked.

I felt this question sufficiently answered when my companion murmured in a musing, almost envious way: "Oh, but she loves them—she loves them!"

This reflexion, repeated with such emphasis, gave me great comfort; but to obtain more of that balm I said: "If she shouldn't intend to destroy the objects we speak of before her death she'll probably have made some disposition by will."

"By will?"

"Hasn't she made a will for your benefit?"

"Ah, she has so little to leave. That's why she likes money," said Miss Tina.

"Might I ask, since we're really talking things over, what you and she live on?"

"On some money that comes from America, from a gentleman—I think a lawyer—in New York. He sends it every quarter. £It isn't much!"

"And won't she have disposed of that?"

My companion hesitated—I saw she was blushing. "I believe it's mine," she said; and the look and tone which accompanied these words betrayed so the absence of the habit of thinking of herself that I almost thought her charming. The next instant she added: "But she had in an *avvocato* here once, ever so long ago. And some people came and signed something."

"They were probably witnesses. And you weren't asked to sign? Well then," I argued, rapidly and hopefully, "it's because you're the legatee. She must have left all her documents to you!"

"If she has it's with very strict conditions," Miss Tina responded, rising quickly, while the movement gave the words a small character of decision. They seemed to imply that the bequest would be accompanied with a proviso that the articles bequeathed should remain concealed from every inquisitive eye, and that I was very much mistaken if I thought her the person to depart from an injunction so absolute.

"Oh, of course, you'll have to abide by the terms," I said; and she uttered nothing to mitigate the rigour of this conclusion. None the less, later on, just before we disembarked at her own door after a return which had taken place almost in silence, she said to me abruptly: "I'll do what I can to help you." I was grateful for this—it was very well so far as it went; but it didn't keep me from remembering that night in a worried waking hour that I now had her word for it to re-enforce my own impression that the old woman was full of craft.

VII

THE fear of what this side of her character might have led her to do made me nervous for days afterwards. I waited for an intimation from Miss Tina; I almost read it as her duty to keep me informed, to let me know definitely whether or no Miss Bordereau had sacrificed her treasures. But as she gave no sign I lost patience and determined to put the case to the very touch of my own senses. I sent late one afternoon to ask if I might pay the ladies a visit, and my servant came back with surprising news. Miss Bordereau could be approached without the least difficulty; she had been moved out into the *sala* and was sitting by the window that overlooked the garden. I descended and found this picture correct; the old lady had been wheeled forth into the world and had a certain air, which came mainly perhaps from some brighter element in her dress, of being prepared again to have converse with it. It had not yet, however, begun to flock about her; she was perfectly alone and, though the door leading to her own quarters stood open, I had at first no glimpse of Miss Tina. The window at which she sat had the afternoon shade and, one of the shutters having been pushed back, she could see the pleasant garden, where the summer sun had by this time dried up too many of the plants—she could see the yellow light and the long shadows.

"Have you come to tell me you'll take the rooms for six months more?" she asked as I approached her, startling me by something coarse in her cupidity almost as much as if she hadn't already given me a specimen of it. Juliana's desire to make our acquaintance lucrative had been, as I have sufficiently indicated, a false note in my image of the woman who had inspired a great poet with immortal lines; but I may say here definitely that I after all recognised large allowance to be made for her. It was I who had kindled the unholy flame; it was I who had put into her head that she had the means of making money. She appeared never to have thought of that; she had been living wastefully for years, in a house five times too big for her, on a footing that I could explain only by the presumption that, excessive as it was, the space she enjoyed cost her next to nothing and that, small as were her revenues, they left her, for Venice, an appreciable margin. I had descended on her one day and taught her to calculate, and my almost extravagant comedy on the subject of the garden had presented me irresistibly in the light of a victim. Like all persons who achieve the miracle of changing their point of view late in life, she had been intensely converted: she had seized my hint with a desperate tremulous clutch.

I invited myself to go and get one of the chairs that stood, at a distance, against the wall—she had given herself no concern as to whether I should sit or stand; and while I placed it near her I began gaily: "Oh, dear madam, what an imagination you have, what an intellectual sweep! I'm a poor devil of a man of letters who lives from day to day. How can I take palaces by the year? My existence is precarious. I don't know whether six months hence I shall have bread to put in my mouth. I've treated myself for once; it has been an immense luxury. But when it comes to going on——!"

"Are your rooms too dear? If they are you can have more for the same money," Juliana responded. "We can arrange, we can *combinare*, as they say here."

"Well, yes, since you ask me, they're too dear, much too dear," I said. "Evidently you suppose me richer than I am."

She looked at me as from the mouth of her cave. "If you write books don't you sell them?"

"Do you mean don't people buy them? A little, a very little— not so much as I could wish. Writing books, unless one be a great genius—and even then!—is the last road to fortune. I think there's no more money to be made by good letters."

"Perhaps you don't choose nice subjects. What do you write about?" Miss Bordereau implacably pursued.

"About the books of other people. I'm a critic, a commentator, an historian, in a small way." I wondered what she was coming to.

"And what other people now?"

"Oh, better ones than myself: the great writers mainly—the great philosophers and poets of the past; those who are dead and gone and can't, poor darlings, speak for themselves."

"And what do you say about them?"

"I say they sometimes attached themselves to very clever women!" I replied as for pleasantness. I had measured, as I thought, my risk, but as my words fell upon the air they were to strike me as imprudent. However, I had launched them and I wasn't sorry, for perhaps after all the old woman would be willing to treat. It seemed tolerably obvious that she knew my secret: why therefore drag the process out? But she didn't take what I had said as a confession; she only asked:

"Do you think it's right to rake up the past?"

"I don't feel that I know what you mean by raking it up. How can we get at it unless we dig a little? The present has such a rough way of treading it down."

"Oh, I like the past, but I don't like critics," my hostess declared with her hard complacency.

"Neither do I, but I like their discoveries."

"Aren't they mostly lies?"

"The lies are what they sometimes discover," I said, smiling at the quiet impertinence of this. "They often lay bare the truth."

"The truth is God's, it isn't man's: we had better leave it alone. Who can judge of it?—who can say?"

"We're terribly in the dark, I know," I admitted; "but if we give up trying what becomes of all the fine things? What becomes of the work I just mentioned, that of the great philosophers and poets? It's all vain words if there's nothing to measure it by."

"You talk as if you were a tailor," said Miss Bordereau whimsically; and then she added quickly and in a different manner: "This house is very fine; the proportions are magnificent. To-day I wanted to look at this part again. I made them bring me out here. When your man came just now to learn if I would see you I was on the point of sending for you to ask if you didn't mean to go on. I wanted to judge what I'm letting you have. This *sala* is very grand," she pursued like an auctioneer, moving a little, as I guessed, her invisible eyes. "I don't believe you often have lived in such a house, eh?"

"I can't often afford to!" I said.

"Well, then, how much will you give me for six months?"

I was on the point of exclaiming—and the air of excruciation in my face would have denoted a moral fact—"Don't, Juliana; for *his* sake, don't!" But I controlled myself and asked less passionately: "Why should I remain so long as that?"

"I thought you liked it," said Miss Bordereau with her shrivelled dignity.

"So I thought I should."

For a moment she said nothing more, and I left my own words to suggest to her what they might. I half-expected her to say, coldly enough, that if I had been disappointed we needn't continue the discussion, and this in spite of the fact that I believed her now to have in her mind—however it had come there—what would have told her that my disappointment was natural. But to my extreme surprise she ended by observing: "If you don't think we've treated you well enough perhaps we can discover some way of treating you better." This speech was somehow so incongruous that it made me laugh again, and I excused myself by saying that she talked as if I were a sulky boy pouting in the corner and having to be "brought round." I hadn't a grain of complaint to make; and could anything have exceeded Miss Tina's graciousness in accompanying me a few nights before to the Piazza? At this the old woman went on: "Well, you brought it on yourself!" And then in a different tone: "She's a very fine girl." I assented cordially to this proposition, and she expressed the hope that I did so not merely to be obliging, but that I really liked her. Meanwhile I wondered still more what Miss Bordereau was coming to. "Except for me, to-day," she said, "she hasn't a relation in the world." Did she by describing her niece as amiable and unencumbered wish to represent her as a *parti*?

It was perfectly true that I couldn't afford to go on with my rooms at a fancy price and that I had already devoted to my undertaking almost all the hard cash I had set apart for it. My patience and my time were by no means exhausted, but I should be able to draw upon them only on a more usual Venetian basis. I was willing to pay the precious personage with whom my pecuniary dealings were such a discord twice as much as any other *padrona di casa* would have asked, but I wasn't willing to pay her twenty times as much. I told her so plainly, and my plainness appeared to have some success, for she exclaimed: "Very good; you've done what I asked—you've made an offer!"

"Yes, but not for half a year. Only by the month."

"Oh, I must think of that then." She seemed disappointed that I wouldn't tie myself to a period, and I guessed that she wished both to secure me and to discourage me; to say severely: "Do you dream that you can get off with less than six months? Do you dream that even by the end of that time you'll be appreciably nearer your victory?" What was most in my mind was that she had a fancy to play me the trick of making me engage myself when in fact she had sacrificed her treasure. There was a moment when my suspense on this point was so acute that I all but broke out with the question, and what kept it back was but an instinctive recoil—lest it should be a mistake—from the last violence of self-exposure. She was such a subtle old witch that one could never tell where one stood with her. You may imagine whether it cleared up the puzzle

when, just after she had said she would think of my proposal and
without any formal transition, she drew out of her pocket with an
embarrassed hand a small object wrapped in crumpled white
paper. She held it there a moment and then resumed: "Do you
know much about curiosities?"

"About curiosities?"

"About antiquities, the old gimcracks that people pay so much
for to-day. Do you know the kind of price they bring?"

I thought I saw what was coming, but I said ingenuously: "Do
you want to buy something?"

"No, I want to sell. What would an amateur give me for that?"
She unfolded the white paper and made a motion for me to take
from her a small oval portrait. I possessed myself of it with fingers
of which I could only hope that they didn't betray the intensity of
their clutch, and she added: "I would part with it only for a good
price."

At the first glance I recognised Jeffrey Aspern, and was well
aware that I flushed with the act. As she was watching me, however,
I had the consistency to exclaim: "What a striking face! Do tell me
who he is."

"He's an old friend of mine, a very distinguished man in his
day. He gave it me himself, but I'm afraid to mention his name, lest
you never should have heard of him, critic and historian as you
are. I know the world goes fast and one generation forgets another.
He was all the fashion when I was young."

She was perhaps amazed at my assurance, but I was surprised
at hers; at her having the energy, in her state of health and at her
time of life, to wish to sport with me to that tune simply for her
private entertainment—the humour to test me and practise on me
and befool me. This at least was the interpretation that I put upon
her production of the relic, for I couldn't believe she really desired
to sell it or cared for any information I might give her. What she
wished was to dangle it before my eyes and put a prohibitive price
on it. "The face comes back to me, it torments me," I said, turning
the object this way and that and looking at it very critically. It was
a careful but not a supreme work of art, larger than the ordinary
miniature and representing a young man with a remarkably hand-

some face, in a high-collared green coat and a buff waistcoat. I felt in the little work a virtue of likeness and judged it to have been painted when the model was about twenty-five. There are, as all the world knows, three other portraits of the poet in existence, but none of so early a date as this elegant image. "I've never seen the original, clearly a man of a past age, but I've seen other reproductions of this face," I went on. "You expressed doubt of this generation's having heard of the gentleman, but he strikes me for all the world as a celebrity. Now who is he? I can't put my finger on him—I can't give him a label. Wasn't he a writer? Surely he's a poet." I was determined that it should be she, not I, who should first pronounce Jeffrey Aspern's name.

My resolution was taken in ignorance of Miss Bordereau's extremely resolute character, and her lips never formed in my hearing the syllables that meant so much for her. She neglected to answer my question, but raised her hand to take back the picture, using a gesture which though impotent was in a high degree peremptory. "It's only a person who should know for himself that would give me my price," she said with a certain dryness.

"Oh, then you have a price?" I didn't restore the charming thing; not from any vindictive purpose, but because I instinctively clung to it. We looked at each other hard while I retained it.

"I know the least I would take. What it occurred to me to ask you about is the most I shall be able to get."

She made a movement, drawing herself together as if in a spasm of dread at having lost her prize, she had been impelled to the immense effort of rising to snatch it from me. I instantly placed it in her hand again, saying as I did so: "I should like to have it myself, but with your ideas it would be quite beyond my mark."

She turned the small oval plate over in her lap, with its face down, and I heard her catch her breath as after a strain or an escape. This, however, did not prevent her saying in a moment: "You'd buy a likeness of a person you don't know by an artist who has no reputation?"

"The artist may have no reputation, but that thing's wonderfully well painted," I replied, to give myself a reason.

"It's lucky you thought of saying that, because the painter was my father."

"That makes the picture indeed precious!" I returned with
gaiety; and I may add that a part of my cheer came from this proof
I had been right in my theory of Miss Bordereau's origin. Aspern
had of course met the young lady on his going to her father's
studio as a sitter. I observed to Miss Bordereau that if she would
entrust me with her property for twenty-four hours I should be
happy to take advice on it; but she made no other reply than to slip
it in silence into her pocket. This convinced me still more that she
had no sincere intention of selling it during her lifetime, though
she may have desired to satisfy herself as to the sum her niece,
should she leave it to her, might expect eventually to obtain for it.
"Well, at any rate, I hope you won't offer it without giving me
notice," I said as she remained irresponsive. "Remember me as a
possible purchaser."

"I should want your money first!" she returned with unexpected rudeness; and then, as if she bethought herself that I might
well complain of such a tone and wished to turn the matter off,
asked abruptly what I talked about with her niece when I went out
with her that way of an evening.

"You speak as if we had set up the habit," I replied. "Certainly I
should be very glad if it were to become our pleasant custom. But
in that case I should feel a still greater scruple at betraying a lady's
confidence."

"Her confidence? Has my niece confidence?"

"Here she is—she can tell you herself," I said; for Miss Tina
now appeared on the threshold of the old woman's parlour. "Have
you confidence, Miss Tina? Your aunt wants very much to know."

"Not in her, not in her!" the younger lady declared, shaking her
head with a dolefulness that was neither jocular nor affected. "I
don't know what to do with her; she has fits of horrid imprudence.
She's so easily tired—and yet she has begun to roam, to drag
herself about the house." And she looked down at her yoke-fellow
of long years with a vacancy of wonder, as if all their contact and
custom hadn't made her perversities, on occasion, any more easy
to follow.

"I know what I'm about. I'm not losing my mind. I daresay

you'd like to think so," said Miss Bordereau with a crudity of cynicism.

"I don't suppose you came out here yourself. Miss Tina must have had to lend you a hand," I interposed for conciliation.

"Oh, she insisted we should push her; and when she insists!" said Miss Tina, in the same tone of apprehension: as if there were no knowing what service she disapproved of her aunt might force her next to render.

"I've always got most things done I wanted, thank God! The people I've lived with have humoured me," the old woman continued, speaking out of the white ashes of her vanity.

I took it pleasantly up. "I suppose you mean they've obeyed you."

"Well, whatever it is—when they like one."

"It's just because I like you that I want to resist," said Miss Tina with a nervous laugh.

"Oh, I expect you'll bring Miss Bordereau upstairs next to pay me a visit," I went on; to which the old lady replied:

"Oh, no; I can keep an eye on you from here!"

"You're very tired; you'll certainly be ill to-night!" cried Miss Tina.

"Nonsense, dear; I feel better at this moment than I've done for a month. To-morrow I shall come out again. I want to be where I can see this clever gentleman."

"Shouldn't you perhaps see me better in your sitting-room?" I asked.

"Don't you mean shouldn't you have a better chance at *me*?" she returned, fixing me a moment with her green shade.

"Ah, I haven't that anywhere! I look at you but don't see you."

"You agitate her dreadfully—and that's not good," said Miss Tina, giving me a reproachful deterrent headshake.

"I want to watch you—I want to watch you!" Miss Bordereau went on.

"Well, then, let us spend as much of our time together as possible—I don't care where. That will give you every facility."

"Oh, I've seen you enough for to-day. I'm satisfied. Now I'll go home," Juliana said. Miss Tina laid her hands on the back of the

wheeled chair and began to push, but I begged her to let me take
her place. "Oh, yes, you may move me this way—you shan't in any
other!" the old woman cried as she felt herself propelled firmly and
easily over the smooth hard floor. Before we reached the door of
her own apartment she bade me stop, and she took a long last look
up and down the noble *sala*. "Oh, it's a prodigious house!" she
murmured; after which I pushed her forward. When we had
entered the parlour Miss Tina let me know she should now be able
to manage, and at the same moment the little red-haired *donna*
came to meet her mistress. Miss Tina's idea was evidently to get her
aunt immediately back to bed. I confess that in spite of this
urgency I was guilty of the indiscretion of lingering; it held me
there to feel myself so close to the objects I coveted—which would
be probably put away somewhere in the faded unsociable room.
The place had indeed a bareness that suggested no hidden values;
there were neither dusky nooks nor curtained corners, neither
massive cabinets nor chests with iron bands. Moreover it was
possible, it was perhaps even likely, that the old lady had consigned
her relics to her bedroom, to some battered box that was shoved
under the bed, to the drawer of some lame dressing-table, where
they would be in the range of vision by the dim night-lamp. None
the less I turned an eye on every article of furniture, on every
conceivable cover for a hoard, and noticed that there were half a
dozen things with drawers, and in particular a tall old secretary
with brass ornaments of the style of the Empire—a receptacle
somewhat infirm but still capable of keeping rare secrets. I don't
know why this article so engaged me, small purpose as I had of
breaking into it; but I stared at it so hard that Miss Tina noticed me
and changed colour. Her doing this made me think I was right and
that, wherever they might have been before, the Aspern papers at
that moment languished behind the peevish little lock of the
secretary. It was hard to turn my attention from the dull mahogany
front when I reflected that a plain panel divided me from the goal
of my hopes; but I gathered up my slightly scattered prudence and
with an effort took leave of my hostess. To make the effort graceful
I said to her that I should certainly bring her an opinion about the
little picture.

"The little picture?" Miss Tina asked in surprise.

"What do *you* know about it, my dear?" the old woman demanded. "You needn't mind. I've fixed my price."

"And what may that be?"

"A thousand pounds."

"Oh, Lord!" cried poor Miss Tina irrepressibly.

"Is that what she talks to you about?" said Miss Bordereau.

"Imagine your aunt's wanting to know!" I had to separate from my younger friend with only those words, though I should have liked immensely to add: "For heaven's sake meet me to-night in the garden!"

VIII

As it turned out the precaution had not been needed, for three hours later, just as I had finished my dinner, Miss Tina appeared, unannounced, in the open doorway of the room in which my simple repasts were served. I remember well that I felt no surprise at seeing her; which is not a proof of my not believing in her timidity. It was immense, but in a case in which there was a particular reason for boldness it never would have prevented her from running up to my floor. I saw that she was not quite full of a particular reason; it threw her forward—made her seize me, as I rose to meet her, by the arm.

"My aunt's very ill; I think she's dying!"

"Never in the world," I answered bitterly. "Don't you be afraid!"

"Do go for a doctor—do, do! Olimpia's gone for the one we always have, but she doesn't come back; I don't know what has happened to her. I told her that if he wasn't at home she was to follow him where he had gone; but apparently she's following him all over Venice. I don't know what to do—she looks so as if she were sinking."

"May I see her, may I judge?" I asked. "Of course I shall be delighted to bring some one; but hadn't we better send my man instead, so that I may stay with you?"

Miss Tina assented to this and I despatched my servant for the best doctor in the neighbourhood. I hurried downstairs with her, and on the way she told me that an hour after I quitted them in the afternoon Miss Bordereau had had an attack of "oppression," a terrible difficulty in breathing. This had subsided, but had left her so exhausted that she didn't come up; she seemed all spent and gone. I repeated that she wasn't gone, that she wouldn't go yet; whereupon Miss Tina gave me a sharper sidelong glance than she had ever favoured me withal and said: "Really, what do you mean? I suppose you don't accuse her of making-believe!" I forget what reply I made to this, but I fear that in my heart I thought the old woman capable of any weird manœuvre. Miss Tina wanted to know what I had done to her; her aunt had told her I had made her so angry. I declared I had done nothing whatever—I had been exceedingly careful; to which my companion rejoined that our friend had assured her she had had a scene with me—a scene that had upset her. I answered with some resentment that the scene had been of *her* making—that I couldn't think what she was angry with me for unless for not seeing my way to give a thousand pounds for the portrait of Jeffrey Aspern. "And did she show you that? Oh, gracious—oh, deary me!" groaned Miss Tina, who seemed to feel the situation pass out of her control and the elements of her fate thicken round her. I answered her I'd give anything to possess it, yet that I had no thousand pounds; but I stopped when we came to the door of Miss Bordereau's room. I had an immense curiosity to pass it, but I thought it my duty to represent to Miss Tina that if I made the invalid angry she ought perhaps to be spared the sight of me. "The sight of you? Do you think she can *see*?" my companion demanded almost with indignation. I did think so but forebore to say it, and I softly followed my conductress.

I remember that what I said to her as I stood for a moment beside the old woman's bed was: "Does she never show you her eyes then? Have you never seen them?" Miss Bordereau had been divested of her green shade, but—it was not my fortune to behold Juliana in her nightcap—the upper half of her face was covered by the fall of a piece of dingy lace-like muslin, a sort of extemporised

hood which, wound round her head, descended to the end of her
nose, leaving nothing visible but her white withered cheeks and
puckered mouth, closed tightly and, as it were, consciously. Miss
Tina gave me a glance of surprise, evidently not seeing a reason for
my impatience. "You mean she always wears something? She does
it to preserve them."

"Because they're so fine?"

"Oh, to-day, to-day!" And Miss Tina shook her head speaking
very low. "But they used to be magnificent!"

"Yes, indeed—we've Aspern's word for that." And as I looked
again at the old woman's wrappings I could imagine her not
having wished to allow any supposition that the great poet had
overdone it. But I didn't waste my time in considering Juliana, in
whom the appearance of respiration was so slight as to suggest that
no human attention could ever help her more. I turned my eyes
once more all over the room, rummaging with them the closets,
the chests of drawers, the tables. Miss Tina at once noted their
direction and read, I think, what was in them; but she didn't
answer it, turning away restlessly, anxiously, so that I felt rebuked,
with reason, for an appetite well-nigh indecent in the presence of
our dying companion. All the same I took another view, en-
deavouring to pick out mentally the receptacle to try first, for a
person who should wish to put his hand on Miss Bordereau's
papers directly after her death. The place was a dire confusion; it
looked like the dressing-room of an old actress. There were clothes
hanging over chairs, odd-looking shabby bundles here and there,
and various pasteboard boxes piled together, battered, bulging and
discoloured, which might have been fifty years old. Miss Tina after
a moment noticed the direction of my eyes again, and, as if she
guessed how I judged such appearances—forgetting I had no business to judge them at all—said, perhaps to defend herself from the
imputation of complicity in the disorder:

"She likes it this way; we can't move things. There are old band-
boxes she has had most of her life." Then she added, half-taking
pity on my real thought: "Those things were *there*." And she
pointed to a small low trunk which stood under a sofa that just
allowed room for it. It struck me as a queer superannuated coffer,

of painted wood, with elaborate handles and shrivelled straps and
with the colour—it had last been endued with a coat of light
green—much rubbed off. It evidently had travelled with Juliana in
the olden time—in the days of adventures, which it had shared. It
would have made a strange figure arriving at a modern hotel.

"*Were* there—they aren't now?" I asked, startled by Miss Tina's
implication.

She was going to answer, but at that moment the doctor came
in—the doctor whom the little maid had been sent to fetch and
whom she had at last overtaken. My servant, going on his own
errand, had met her with her companion in tow, and in the
sociable Venetian spirit, retracing his steps with them, had also
come up to the threshold of the *padrona*'s room, where I saw him
peep over the doctor's shoulder. I motioned him away the more
instantly that the sight of his prying face reminded me how little I
myself had to do there—an admonition confirmed by the sharp
way the little doctor eyed me, his air of taking me for a rival who
had the field before him. He was a short fat brisk gentleman who
wore the tall hat of his profession and seemed to look at everything
but his patient. He kept me still in range as if it struck him I too
should be better for a dose, so that I bowed to him and left him
with the women, going down to smoke a cigar in the garden. I was
nervous; I couldn't go further; I couldn't leave the place. I don't
know exactly what I thought might happen, but I felt it important
to be there. I wandered about the alleys—the warm night had
come on—smoking cigar after cigar and studying the light in Miss
Bordereau's windows. They were open now, I could see; the situation was different. Sometimes the light moved, but not quickly; it
didn't suggest the hurry of a crisis. Was the old woman dying or
was she already dead? Had the doctor said that there was nothing
to be done at her tremendous age but to let her quietly pass away?
Or had he simply announced with a look a little more conven-
tional that the end of the end had come? Were the other two
women just going and coming over the offices that follow in such
a case? It made me uneasy not to be nearer, as if I thought the
doctor himself might carry away the papers with him. I bit my
cigar hard while it assailed me again that perhaps there were now

no papers to carry!

I wandered about an hour and more. I looked out for Miss Tina at one of the windows, having a vague idea that she might come there to give me some sign. Wouldn't she see the red tip of my cigar in the dark and feel sure I was hanging on to know what the doctor had said? I'm afraid it's a proof of the grossness of my anxieties that I should have taken in some degree for granted at such an hour, in the midst of the greatest change that could fall on her, poor Miss Tina's having also a free mind for them. My servant came down and spoke to me; he knew nothing save that the doctor had gone after a visit of half an hour. If he had stayed half an hour then Miss Bordereau was still alive: it couldn't have taken so long to attest her decease. I sent the man out of the house; there were moments when the sense of his curiosity annoyed me, and this was one of them. *He* had been watching my cigar-tip from an upper window, if Miss Tina hadn't; he couldn't know what I was after and I couldn't tell him, though I suspected in him fantastic private theories about me which he thought fine and which, had I more exactly known them, should have thought offensive.

I went upstairs at last, but I mounted no higher than the *sala*. The door of Miss Bordereau's apartment was open, showing from the parlour the dimness of a poor candle. I went toward it with a light tread, and at the same moment Miss Tina appeared and stood looking at me as I approached. "She's better, she's better," she said even before I had asked. "The doctor has given her something; she woke up, came back to life while he was there. He says there's no immediate danger."

"No immediate danger? Surely he thinks her condition serious."

"Yes, because she had been excited. That affects her dreadfully."

"It will do so again then, because she works herself up. She did so this afternoon."

"Yes, she mustn't come out any more," said Miss Tina with one of her lapses into a deeper detachment.

"What's the use of making such a remark as that," I permitted myself to ask, "if you begin to rattle her about again the first time she bids you?"

"I won't—I won't do it any more."

"You must learn to resist her," I went on.

"Oh, yes, I shall; I shall do so better if you tell me it's right."

"You mustn't do it for me—you must do it for yourself. It all comes back to you, if you're scared and upset."

"Well, I'm not upset now," said Miss Tina placidly enough. "She's very quiet."

"Is she conscious again—does she speak?"

"No, she doesn't speak, but she takes my hand. She holds it fast."

'Yes," I returned, "I can see what force she still has by the way she grabbed that picture this afternoon. But if she holds you fast how comes it that you're here?"

Miss Tina waited a little; though her face was in deep shadow—she had her back to the light in the parlour and I had put down my own candle far off, near the door of the *sala*—I thought I saw her smile ingenuously. "I came on purpose—I had heard your step."

"Why, I came on tiptoe, as soundlessly as possible."

"Well, I had heard you," said Miss Tina.

"And is your aunt alone now?"

"Oh, no—Olimpia sits there."

On my side I debated. "Shall we then pass in there?" And I nodded at the parlour; I wanted more and more to be on the spot. "We can't talk there—she'll hear us."

I was on the point of replying that in that case we'd sit silent, but I felt too much this wouldn't do, there was something I desired so immensely to ask her. Thus I hinted we might walk a little in the *sala*, keeping more at the other end, where we shouldn't disturb our friend. Miss Tina assented unconditionally; the doctor was coming again, she said, and she would be there to meet him at the door. We strolled through the fine superfluous hall, where on the marble floor—particularly as at first we said nothing—our footsteps were more audible than I had expected. When we reached the other end—the wide window, inveterately closed, connecting with the balcony that overhung the canal—I submitted that we had best remain there, as she would see the doctor arrive the sooner. I opened the window and we passed out on the balcony. The air of the canal seemed even heavier, hotter than that of the *sala*. The place was hushed and void; the quiet neighbourhood had gone to sleep. A lamp, here and there, over the narrow black water, glimmered in double; the voice of a man going homeward singing, his jacket on his shoulder and his hat on his ear, came to us from a distance. This didn't prevent the scene from being very *comme il faut*, as Miss Bordereau had called it the first time I saw her. Presently a gondola passed along the canal with its slow rhythmical plash, and as we listened we watched it in silence. It didn't stop, it didn't carry the doctor; and after it had gone on I said to Miss Tina:

"And where are they now—the things that were in the trunk?"

"In the trunk?"

"That green box you pointed out to me in her room. You said her papers had been there; you seemed to mean she had transferred them."

"Oh, yes; they're not in the trunk," said Miss Tina.

"May I ask if you've looked?"

"Yes, I've looked—for you."

"How for me, dear Miss Tina? Do you mean you'd have given them to me if you had found them?"—and I fairly trembled with the question.

She delayed to reply and I waited. Suddenly she broke out: "I don't know what I'd do—what I wouldn't!"

"Would you look again—somewhere else?"

She had spoken with a strange unexpected emotion, and she went on in the same tone: "I can't—I can't—while she lies there. It isn't decent."

"No, it isn't decent," I replied gravely. "Let the poor lady rest in peace." And the words, on my lips, were not hypocritical, for I felt reprimanded and shamed.

Miss Tina added in a moment, as if she had guessed this and were sorry for me, but at the same time wished to explain that I did push her, or at least harp on the chord, too much: "I can't deceive her that way. I can't deceive her—perhaps on her deathbed."

"Heaven forbid I should ask you, though I've been guilty

myself!"

"You've been guilty?"

"I've sailed under false colours." I felt now I must make a clean breast of it, must tell her I had given her an invented name on account of my fear her aunt would have heard of me and so refuse to take me in. I explained this as well as that I had really been a party to the letter addressed them by John Cumnor months before.

She listened with great attention, almost in fact gaping for wonder, and when I had made my confession she said: "Then your real name—what is it?" She repeated it over twice when I had told her, accompanying it with the exclamation, "Gracious, gracious!" Then she added: "I like your own best."

"So do I"—and I felt my laugh rueful. "Ouf! it's a relief to get rid of the other."

"So it was a regular plot—a kind of conspiracy?"

"Oh, a conspiracy—we were only two," I replied, leaving out of course Mrs. Prest.

She considered; I thought she was perhaps going to pronounce us very base. But this was not her way, and she remarked after a moment, as in candid impartial contemplation: "How much you must want them!"

"Oh, I do, passionately!" I grinned, I fear, to admit. And this chance made me go on, forgetting my compunction of a moment before. "How can she possibly have changed their place herself? How can she walk? How can she arrive at that sort of muscular exertion? How can she lift and carry things?"

"Oh, when one wants and when one has so much will!" said Miss Tina as if she had thought over my question already herself and had simply had no choice but that answer—the idea that in the dead of night, or at some moment when the coast was clear, the old woman had been capable of a miraculous effort.

"Have you questioned Olimpia? Hasn't she helped her—hasn't she done it for her?" I asked; to which my friend replied promptly and positively that their servant had had nothing to do with the matter, though without admitting definitely that she had spoken to her. It was as if she were a little shy, a little ashamed now, of letting me see how much she had entered into my uneasiness and had me on her mind. Suddenly she said to me without any immediate relevance:

"I rather feel you a new person, you know, now that you've a new name."

"It isn't a new one; it's a very good old one, thank fortune!"

She looked at me a moment. "Well, I do like it better."

"Oh, if you didn't I would almost go on with the other!"

"Would you really?"

I laughed again, but I returned for all answer: "Of course if she can rummage about that way she can perfectly have burnt them."

"You must wait—you must wait," Miss Tina mournfully moralised; and her tone ministered little to my patience, for it seemed after all to accept that wretched possibility. I would teach myself to wait, I declared nevertheless; because in the first place I couldn't do otherwise and in the second I had her promise, given me the other night, that she would help me.

"Of course if the papers are gone that's no use," she said; not as if she wished to recede, but only to be conscientious.

"Naturally. But if you could only find out!" I groaned, quivering again.

"I thought you promised you'd wait."

"Oh, you mean wait even for that?"

"For what then?"

"Ah, nothing," I answered rather foolishly, being ashamed to tell her what had been implied in my acceptance of delay—the idea that she would perhaps do more for me than merely find out.

I know not if she guessed this; at all events she seemed to bethink herself of some propriety of showing me more rigour. "I didn't promise to deceive, did I? I don't think I did."

"It doesn't much matter whether you did or not, for you couldn't!"

Nothing is more possible than that she wouldn't have contested this even hadn't she been diverted by our seeing the doctor's gondola shoot into the little canal and approach the house. I noted that he came as fast as if he believed our proprietress still in danger. We looked down at him while he disembarked and then went back into the sala to meet him. When he came up, however, I naturally left Miss Tina to go off with him alone, only asking her leave to come back later for news.

I went out of the house and walked far, as far as the Piazza, where my restlessness declined to quit me. I was unable to sit down; it was very late now though there were people still at the little tables in front of the cafés: I could but uneasily revolve, and I did so half a dozen times. The only comfort, none the less, was in my having told Miss Tina who I really was. At last I took my way home again, getting gradually and all but inextricably lost, as I did whenever I went out in Venice: so that it was considerably past midnight when I reached my door. The *sala*, upstairs, was as dark as usual, and my lamp as I crossed it found nothing satisfactory to show me. I was disappointed, for I had notified Miss Tina that I would come back for a report, and I thought she might have left a light there as a sign. The door of the ladies' apartment was closed; which seemed a hint that my faltering friend had gone to bed in impatience of waiting for me. I stood in the middle of the place, considering, hoping she would hear me and perhaps peep out, saying to myself too that she would never go to bed with her aunt in a state so critical; she would sit up and watch—she would be in a chair, in her dressing-gown. I went nearer the door; I stopped there and listened. I heard nothing at all and at last I tapped gently. No answer came, and after another minute I turned the handle. There was no light in the room; this ought to have prevented my entrance, but it had no such effect. If I have frankly stated the importunities, the indelicacies, of which my desire to possess myself of Jeffrey Aspern's papers had made me capable I needn't shrink, it seems to me, from confessing this last indiscretion. I regard it as the worst thing I did, yet there were extenuating circumstances. I was deeply though doubtless not disinterestedly anxious for more news of Juliana, and Miss Tina had accepted from me, as it were, a rendezvous which it might have been a point of honour with me to keep. It may be objected that her leaving the place dark was a positive sign that she released me, and to this I can only reply that I whished not to be released.

The door of Miss Bordereau's room was open and I could see

beyond it the faintness of a taper. There was no sound—my
footstep caused no one to stir. I came farther into the room; I
lingered there lamp in hand. I wanted to give Miss Tina a chance to
come to me if, as I couldn't doubt, she were still with her aunt. I
made no noise to call her; I only waited to see if she wouldn't
notice my light. She didn't, and I explained this—I found afterwards I was right—by the idea that she had fallen asleep. If she had
fallen asleep her aunt was not on her mind, and my explanation
ought to have led me to go out as I had come. I must repeat again
that it didn't, for I found myself at the same moment given up to
something else. I had no definite purpose, no bad intention, but
felt myself held to the spot by an acute, though absurd, sense of
opportunity. Opportunity for what I couldn't have said, inasmuch
as it wasn't in my mind that I might proceed to thievery. Even had
this tempted me I was confronted with the evident fact that Miss
Bordereau didn't leave her secretary, her cupboard and the drawers
of her tables gaping. I had no keys, no tools and no ambition to
smash her furniture. None the less it came to me that I was now,
perhaps, alone, unmolested, at the hour of freedom and safety,
nearer to the source of my hopes than I had ever been. I held up my
lamp, let the light play on the different objects as if it could tell me
something. Still there came no movement from the other room. If
Miss Tina was sleeping she was sleeping sound. Was she doing
so—generous creature—on purpose to leave me the field? Did she
know I was there and was she just keeping quiet to see what I
would do—what I *could* do? Yet might I, when it came to that? She
herself knew even better than I how little.

I stopped in front of the secretary, gaping at it vainly and no
doubt grotesquely; for what had it to say to me after all? In the first
place it was locked, and in the second it almost surely contained
nothing in which I was interested. Ten to one the papers had been
destroyed, and even if they hadn't the keen old woman wouldn't
have put them in such a place as that after removing them from the
green trunk—wouldn't have transferred them, with the idea of
their safety on her brain, from the better hiding-place to the worse.
The secretary was more conspicuous, more exposed in a room in
which she could no longer mount guard. It opened with a key, but

there was a small brass handle, like a button, as well: I saw this as I played my lamp over it. I did something more, for the climax of my crisis; I caught a glimpse of the possibility that Miss Tina wished me really to understand. If she didn't so wish me, if she wished me to keep away, why hadn't she locked the door of communication between the sitting-room and the *sala*? That would have been a definite sign that I was to leave them alone. If I didn't leave them alone she meant me to come for a purpose—a purpose now represented by the super-subtle inference that to oblige me she had unlocked the secretary. She hadn't left the key, but the lid would probably move if I touched the button. This possibility pressed me hard and I bent very close to judge. I didn't propose to do anything, not even—not in the least—to let down the lid; I only wanted to test my theory, to see if the cover *would* move. I touched the button with my hand—a mere touch would tell me; and as I did so—it is embarrassing for me to relate it—I looked over my shoulder. It was a chance, an instinct, for I had really heard nothing. I almost let my luminary drop and certainly I stepped back, straightening myself up at what I saw. Juliana stood there in her night-dress, by the doorway of her room, watching me; her hands were raised, she had lifted the everlasting curtain that covered half her face, and for the first, the last, the only time I beheld her extraordinary eyes. They glared at me; they were like the sudden drench, for a caught burglar, of a flood of gaslight; they made me horribly ashamed. I never shall forget her strange little bent white tottering figure, with its lifted head, her attitude, her expression; neither shall I forget the tone in which as I turned, looking at her, she hissed out passionately, furiously:

"Ah, you publishing scoundrel!"

I can't now say what I stammered to excuse myself, to explain; but I went toward her to tell her I meant no harm. She waved me off with her old hands, retreating before me in horror; and the next thing I knew she had fallen back with a quick spasm, as if death had descended on her, into Miss Tina's arms.

IX

I LEFT Venice the next morning, directly on learning that my hostess had not succumbed, as I feared at the moment, to the shock I had given her—the shock I may also say she had given me. How in the world could I have supposed her capable of getting out of bed by herself? I failed to see Miss Tina before going; I only saw the *donna*, whom I entrusted with a note for her younger mistress. In this note I mentioned that I should be absent but a few days. I went to Treviso, to Bassano, to Castelfranco; I took walks and drives and looked at musty old churches with ill-lighted pictures; I spent hours seated smoking at the doors of cafés, where there were flies and yellow curtains, on the shady side of sleepy little squares. In spite of these pastimes, which were mechanical and perfunctory, I scantly enjoyed my travels: I had had to gulp down a bitter draught and couldn't get ride of the taste. I had been devilish awkward, as the young men say, to be found by Juliana in the dead of night examining the attachment of her bureau; and it had not been less so to have to believe for a good many hours after that it was highly probable I had killed her. My humiliation galled me, but I had to make the best of it, had, in writing to Miss Tina, to minimise it, as well as account for the posture in which I had been discovered. As she gave me no word of answer I couldn't know what impression I made on her. It rankled for me that I had been called a publishing scoundrel, since certainly I did publish and no less certainly hadn't been very delicate. There was a moment when I stood convinced that the only way to purge my dishonour was to take myself straight away on the instant; to sacrifice my hopes and relieve the two poor women for ever of the oppression of my intercourse. Then I reflected that I had better try a short absence first, for I must already have had a sense (unexpressed and dim) that in disappearing completely it wouldn't be merely my own hopes I should condemn to extinction. It would perhaps answer if I kept

dark long enough to give the elder lady time to believe herself rid
of me. That she would wish to be rid of me after this—if I wasn't
rid of her—was now not to be doubted: that midnight monstrosity
would have cured her of the disposition to put up with my
company for the sake of my dollars. I said to myself that after all I
couldn't abandon Miss Tina, and I continued to say this even while
I noted that she quite ignored my earnest request—I had given her
two or three addresses, at little towns, *poste restante*—for some
sign of her actual state. I would have made my servant write me
news but that he was unable to manage a pen. Couldn't I measure
the scorn of Miss Tina's silence—little disdainful as she had ever
been? Really the soreness pressed; yet if I had scruples about going
back I had others about not doing so, and I wanted to put myself
on a better footing. The end of it was that I did return to Venice on
the twelfth day; and as my gondola gently bumped against our
palace steps a fine palpitation of suspense showed me the violence
my absence had done me.

I had faced about so abruptly that I hadn't even telegraphed to
my servant. He was therefore not at the station to meet me, but he
poked out his head from an upper window when I reached the
house. "They have put her into earth, *quella vecchia*," he said to me
in the lower hall while he shouldered my valise; and he grinned
and almost winked as if he knew I should be pleased with his news.

"She's dead!" I cried, giving him a very different look.

"So it appears, since they've buried her."

"It's all over then? When was the funeral?"

"The other yesterday. But a funeral you could scarcely call it,
signore: *roba da niente—un piccolo passeggio brutto* of two
gondolas. *Poveretta!*" the man continued, referring apparently to
Miss Tina. His conception of funerals was that they were mainly to
amuse the living.

I wanted to know about Miss Tina, how she might be and
generally where; but I asked him no more questions till we had got
upstairs. Now that the fact had met me I took a bad view of it, especially of the idea that poor Miss Tina had had to manage by herself
after the end. What did she know about arrangements, about the
steps to take in such a case? *Poveretta* indeed! I could only hope the

doctor had given her support and that she hadn't been neglected by the old friends of whom she had told me, the little band of the faithful whose fidelity consisted in coming to the house once a year. I elicited from my servant that two old ladies and an old gentleman had in fact rallied round Miss Tina and had supported her—they had come for her in a gondola of their own—during the journey to the cemetery, the little red-walled island of tombs which lies to the north of the town and on the way to Murano. It appeared from these signs that the Misses Bordereau were Catholics, a discovery I had never made, as the old woman couldn't go to church and her niece, so far as I perceived, either didn't, or went only to early mass in the parish before I was stirring. Certainly even the priests respected their seclusion; I had never caught the whisk of the *curato*'s skirt. That evening, an hour later, I sent my servant down with five words on a card to ask if Miss Tina would see me a few moments. She was not in the house, where he had sought her, he told me when he came back, but in the garden walking about to refresh herself and picking the flowers quite as if they belonged to her. He had found her there and she would be happy to see me.

I went down and passed half an hour with poor Miss Tina. She had always had a look of musty mourning, as if she were wearing out old robes of sorrow that wouldn't come to an end; and in this particular she made no different show. But she clearly had been crying, crying a great deal—simply, satisfyingly, refreshingly, with a primitive retarded sense of solitude and violence. But she had none of the airs or graces of grief, and I was almost surprised to see her stand there in the first dusk with her hands full of admirable roses and smile at me with reddened eyes. Her white face, in the frame of her mantilla, looked longer, leaner than usual. I hadn't doubted her being irreconcilably disgusted with me, her considering I ought to have been on the spot to advise her, to help her; and, though I believed there was no rancour in her composition and no great conviction of the importance of her affairs, I had prepared myself for a change in her manner, for some air of injury and estrangement, which should say to my conscience: "Well, you're a nice person to have professed things!" But historic truth compels me to declare that this poor lady's dull face ceased to be dull, almost ceased to be plain, as she turned it gladly to her late aunt's lodger. That touched him extremely, and he thought it simplified his situation until he found it didn't. I was as kind to her that evening as I knew how to be, and I walked about the garden with her as long as seemed good. There was no explanation of any sort between us; I didn't ask her why she hadn't answered my letter. Still less did I repeat what I had said to her in that communication; if she chose to let me suppose she had forgotten the position in which Miss Bordereau had surprised me and the effect of the discovery on the old woman, I was quite willing to take it that way: I was grateful to her for not treating me as if I had killed her aunt.

We strolled and strolled, though really not much passed between us save the recognition of her bereavement, conveyed in my manner and in the expression she had of depending on me now, since I let her see I still took an interest in her. Miss Tina's was no breast for the pride or the pretence of independence; she didn't in the least suggest that she knew at present what would become of her. I forbore to press on that question, however, for I certainly was not prepared to say that I would take charge of her. I was cautious; not ignobly, I think, for I felt her knowledge of life to be so small that in her unsophisticated vision there would be no reason why— since I seemed to pity her—I shouldn't somehow look after her. She told me how her aunt had died, very peacefully at the last, and how everything had been done afterwards by the care of her good friends—fortunately, thanks to me, she said, smiling, there was money in the house. She repeated that when once the "nice" Italians like you they are your friends for life, and when we had gone into this she asked me about my *giro*, my impressions, my adventures, the places I had seen. I told her what I could, making it up partly, I'm afraid, as in my disconcerted state I had taken little in; and after she had heard me she exclaimed, quite as if she had forgotten her aunt and her sorrow, "Dear, dear, how much I should like to do such things—to take an amusing little journey!" It came over me for the moment that I ought to propose some enterprise, say I would accompany her anywhere she liked; and I remarked at any rate that a pleasant excursion—to give her a change—might be managed: we would think of it, talk it over. I spoke never a word of the Aspern documents, asked no question as to what she had ascertained or what had otherwise happened with regard to them before Juliana's death. It wasn't that I wasn't on pins and needles to know, but that I thought it more decent not to show greed again so soon after the catastrophe. I hoped she herself would say something, but she never glanced that way, and I thought this natural at the time. Later on, however, that night, it occurred to me that her silence was matter for suspicion; since if she had talked of my movements, of anything so detached as the Giorgione at Castelfranco, she might have alluded to what she could easily remember was in my mind. It was not to be supposed the emotion produced by her aunt's death had blotted out the recollection that I was interested in that lady's relics, and I fidgeted afterwards as it came to me that her reticence might very possibly just mean that no relics survived. We separated in the garden—it was she who said she must go in; now that she was alone on the *piano nobile* I felt that (judged at any rate by Venetian ideas) I was on rather a different footing in regard to the invasion of it. As I shook hands with her for good-night I asked if she had some general plan, had thought over what she had best do. "Oh yes, oh yes, but I haven't settled anything yet," she replied quite cheerfully. Was her cheerfulness explained by the impression that I would settle for her?

I was glad the next morning that we had neglected practical questions, as this gave me a pretext for seeing her again immediately. There was a practical enough question now to be touched on. I owed it to her to let her know formally that of course I didn't expect her to keep me on as a lodger, as also to show some interest in her own tenure, what she might have on her hands in the way of a lease. But I was not destined, as befell, to converse with her for more than an instant on either of these points. I sent her no message; I simply went down to the *sala* and walked to and fro there. I knew she would come out; she would promptly see me accessible. Somehow I preferred not to be shut up with her; gardens and big halls seemed better places to talk. It was a splendid morning, with something in the air that told of the waning of the long Venetian summer; a freshness from the sea that stirred the flowers in the garden and made a pleasant draught in the house, less shuttered and darkened now than when the old woman was alive. It was the beginning of autumn, of the end of the golden months. With this it was the end of my experiment—or would be in the course of half an hour, when I should really have learned that my dream had been reduced to ashes. After that there would be nothing left for me but to go to the station; for seriously—and as it struck me in the morning light—I couldn't linger there to act as guardian to a piece of middle-aged female helplessness. If she hadn't saved the papers wherein should I be indebted to her? I think I winced a little as I asked myself how much, if she *had* saved them, I should have to recognise and, as it were, reward such a courtesy. Mightn't that service after all saddle me with a guardianship? If this idea didn't make me more uncomfortable as I walked up and down it was because I was convinced I had nothing to look to. If the old woman hadn't destroyed everything before she pounced on me in the parlour she had done so the next day.

It took Miss Tina rather longer than I had expected to act on my calculation; but when at last she came out she looked at me without surprise. I mentioned I had been waiting for her and she asked why I hadn't let her know. I was glad a few hours later on that I had checked myself before remarking that a friendly intuition might have told her: it turned to comfort for me that I hadn't played even to that mild extent on her sensibility. What I did say was virtually the truth—that I was too nervous, since I expected her now to settle my fate.

"Your fate?" said Miss Tina, giving me a queer look; and as she spoke I noticed a rare change in her. Yes, she was other than she had been the evening before—less natural and less easy. She had been crying the day before and was not crying now, yet she struck me as less confident. It was as if something had happened to her during the night, or at least as if she had thought of something that troubled her—something in particular that affected her relations with me, made them more embarrassing and more complicated. Had she simply begun to feel that her aunt's not being there now altered my position?

"I mean about our papers. *Are* there any? You must know now."

"Yes, there are a great many; more than I supposed." I was struck with the way her voice trembled as she told me this.

"Do you mean you've got them in there—and that I may see them?"

"I don't think you can see them," said Miss Tina with an extraordinary expression of entreaty in her eyes, as if the dearest hope she had in the world now was that I wouldn't take them from her. But how could she expect me to make such a sacrifice as that after all that had passed between us? What had I come back to Venice for but to see them, to take them? My joy at learning they were still in existence was such that if the poor woman had gone down on her knees to beseech me never to mention them again I would have treated the proceeding as a bad joke. "I've got them but I can't show them," she lamentably added.

"Not even to me? Ah, Miss Tina!" I broke into a tone of infinite remonstrance and reproach.

She coloured and the tears came back to her eyes; I measured the anguish it cost her to take such a stand, which a dreadful sense of duty had imposed on her. It made me quite sick to find myself confronted with that particular obstacle; all the more that it seemed to me I had been distinctly encouraged to leave it out of account. I quite held Miss Tina to have assured me that if she had no greater hindrance than that——! "You don't mean to say you made her a deathbed promise? It was precisely against your doing anything of that sort that I thought I was safe. Oh I would rather she had burnt the papers outright than have to reckon with such a treachery as that."

"No, it isn't a promise," said Miss Tina.

"Pray what is it then?"

She hung fire, but finally said: "She tried to burn them, but I prevented it. She had hid them in her bed."

"In her bed——?"

"Between the mattresses. That's where she put them when she took them out of the trunk. I can't understand how she did it, because Olimpia didn't help her. She tells me so and I believe her. My aunt only told her afterwards, so that she shouldn't undo the bed—anything but the sheets. So it was very badly made," added Miss Tina simply.

"I should think so! And how did she try to burn them?"

"She didn't try much; she was too weak those last days. But she told me—she charged me. Oh, it was terrible! She couldn't speak after that night. She could only make signs."

"And what did you do?"

"I took them away. I locked them up."

"In the secretary?"

"Yes, in the secretary," said Miss Tina, reddening again.

"Did you tell her you'd burn them?"

"No, I didn't—on purpose."

"On purpose to gratify me?"

"Yes, only for that."

"And what good will you have done me if after all you won't show them?"

"Oh, none. I know that—I know that," she dismally sounded.

"And did she believe you had destroyed them?"

"I don't know what she believed at the last. I couldn't tell—she was too far gone."

"Then if there was no promise and no assurance I can't see what ties you."

"Oh, she hated it so—she hated it so! She was so jealous. But here's the portrait—you may have that" the poor woman announced, taking the little picture, wrapped up in the same manner in which her aunt had wrapped it, out of her pocket.

"I may have it—do you mean you give it to me?" I gasped as it passed into my hand.

"Oh, yes."

"But it's worth money—a large sum."

"Well!" said Miss Tina, still with her strange look.

I didn't know what to make of it, for it could scarcely mean that she wanted to bargain like her aunt. She spoke as for making me a present. "I can't take it from you as a gift," I said, "and yet I can't afford to pay you for it according to the idea Miss Bordereau had of its value. She rated it at a thousand pounds."

"Couldn't we sell it?" my friend threw off.

"God forbid! I prefer the picture to the money."

"Well, then, keep it."

"You're very generous."

"So are you."

"I don't know why you should think so," I returned; and this was true enough, for the good creature appeared to have it in her mind some rich reference that I didn't in the least seize.

"Well, you've made a great difference for me," she said.

I looked at Jeffrey Aspern's face in the little picture, partly in order not to look at that of my companion, which had begun to trouble me, even to frighten me a little—it had taken so very odd, so strained and unnatural a cast. I made no answer to this last declaration; I but privately consulted Jeffrey Aspern's delightful eyes with my own—they were so young and brilliant and yet so wise and so deep: I asked him what on earth was the matter with Miss Tina. He seemed to smile at me with mild mockery; he might have been amused at my case. I had got into a pickle for him—as if he needed it! He was unsatisfactory for the only moment since I had known him. Nevertheless, now that I held the little picture in my hand I felt it would be a precious possession. "Is this a bribe to make me give up the papers?" I presently and all perversely asked. "Much as I value this, you know, if I were to be obliged to choose, the papers are what I should prefer. Ah but ever so much!"

"How can you choose—how can you choose?" Miss Tina returned slowly and woefully.

"I see! Of course there's nothing to be said if you regard the interdiction that rests on you as quite insurmountable. In this case it must seem to you that to part with them would be an impiety of the worst kind, a simple sacrilege!"

She shook her head, only lost in the queerness of her case. "You'd understand if you had known her. I'm afraid," she quavered suddenly—"I'm afraid! She was terrible when she was angry."

"Yes, I saw something of that, that night. She was terrible. Then I saw her eyes. Lord, they were fine!"

"I see them—they stare at me in the dark!" said Miss Tina.

"You've grown nervous with all you've been through."

"Oh, yes, very—very!"

"You mustn't mind; that will pass away," I said kindly. Then I added resignedly, for it really seemed to me that I must accept the situation: "Well, so it is, and it can't be helped. I must renounce." My friend, at this, with her eyes on me, gave a low soft moan, and I went on: "I only wish to goodness she had destroyed them: then there would be nothing more to say. And I can't understand why, with her ideas, she didn't."

"Oh, she lived on them!" said Miss Tina.

"You can imagine whether that makes me want less to see them," I returned not quite so desperately. "But don't let me stand here as if I had it in my soul to tempt you to anything base. Naturally, you understand, I give up my rooms. I leave Venice immediately." And I took up my hat, which I had placed on a chair. We were still rather awkwardly on our feet in the middle of the sala. She had left the door of the apartments open behind her, but had not led me that way.

A strange spasm came into her face as she saw me take my hat. "Immediately—do you mean to-day?" The tone of the words was tragic—they were a cry of desolation.

"Oh, no; not so long as I can be of the least service to you."

"Well, just a day or two more—just two or three days," she panted. Then controlling herself she added in another manner: "She wanted to say something to me—the last day—something very particular. But she couldn't."

"Something very particular?"

"Something more about the papers."

"And did you guess—have you any idea?"

"No, I've tried to think—but I don't know. I've thought all kinds of things."

"As for instance?"

"Well, that if you were a relation it would be different."

I wondered. "If I were a relation——?"

"If you weren't a stranger. Then it would be the same for you as for me. Anything that's mine would be yours, and you could do what you like. I shouldn't be able to prevent you—and you'd have no responsibility."

She brought out this droll explanation with a nervous rush and as if speaking words got by heart. They gave me the impression of a subtlety which at first I failed to follow. But after a moment her face helped me to see farther, and then the queerest of lights came to me. It was embarrassing, and I bent my head over Jeffrey Aspern's portrait. What an odd expression was in his face! "Get out of it as you can, my dear fellow!" I put the picture into the pocket of my coat and said to Miss Tina: "Yes, I'll sell it for you. I shan't get a thousand pounds by any means, but I shall get something good."

She looked at me through pitiful tears, but seemed to try to smile as she returned: "We can divide the money."

"No, no, it shall be all yours." Then I went on: "I think I know what your poor aunt wanted to say. She wanted to give directions that her papers should be buried with her."

Miss Tina appeared to weigh this suggestion; after which she answered with striking decision, "Oh no, she wouldn't have thought that safe!"

"It seems to me nothing could be safer."

"She had an idea that when people want to publish they're capable——!" And she paused, very red.

"Of violating a tomb? Mercy on us, what must she have thought of me!"

"She wasn't just, she wasn't generous!" my companion cried with sudden passion.

The light that had come into my mind a moment before spread farther. "Ah, don't say that, for we *are* a dreadful race." Then I pursued: "If she left a will that may give you some idea."

"I've found nothing of the sort—she destroyed it. She was very fond of me," Miss Tina added with an effect of extreme inconsequence. "She wanted me to be happy. And if any person should be kind to me—she wanted to speak of that."

I was almost awestricken by the astuteness with which the good lady found herself inspired, transparent astuteness as it was and stitching, as the phrase is, with white thread. "Depend upon it she didn't want to make any provision that would be agreeable to *me*."

"No, not to you, but quite to me. She knew I should like it if you could carry out your idea. Not because she cared for you, but because she did think of me," Miss Tina went on with her unexpected persuasive volubility. "You could see the things—you could use them." She stopped, seeing I grasped the sense of her conditional—stopped long enough for me to give some sign that I didn't give. She must have been conscious, however, that though my face showed the greatest embarrassment ever painted on a human countenance it was not set as a stone, it was also full of compassion. It was a comfort to me a long time afterwards to consider that she couldn't have seen in me the smallest symptom of disrespect. "I don't know what to do; I'm too tormented, I'm too ashamed!" she continued with vehemence. Then turning away from me and burying her face in her hands she burst into a flood of tears. If she didn't know what to do it may be imagined whether I knew better. I stood there dumb, watching her while her sobs resounded in the great empty hall. In a moment she was up at me again with her streaming eyes. "I'd give you everything, and she'd understand, where she is—she'd forgive me!"

"Ah, Miss Tina—ah, Miss Tina," I stammered for all reply. I didn't know what to do, as I say, but at a venture I made a wild vague movement in consequence of which I found myself at the door. I remember standing there and saying, "It wouldn't do, it wouldn't do!"—saying it pensively, awkwardly, grotesquely, while I looked away to the opposite end of the sala as at something very interesting. The next thing I remember is that I was downstairs and out of the house. My gondola was there and my gondolier, reclining on the cushions, sprang up as soon as he saw me. I jumped in and to his usual "*Dove commanda?*" replied, in a tone that made him stare: "Anywhere, anywhere; out into the lagoon!"

He rowed me away and I sat there prostrate, groaning softly to myself, my hat pulled over my brow. What in the name of the preposterous did she mean if she didn't mean to offer me her hand? That was the price—that was the price! And did she think I wanted it, poor deluded infatuated extravagant lady? My gondolier, behind me, must have seen my ears red as I wondered, motionless there under the fluttering *tenda* with my hidden face, noticing nothing as we passed—wondered whether her delusion, her infatuation had been my own reckless work. Did she think I had made love to her even to get the papers? I hadn't, I hadn't; I repeated that over to myself for an hour, for two hours, till I was wearied if not convinced. I don't know where, on the lagoon, my gondolier took me; we floated aimlessly and with slow rare strokes. At last I became conscious that we were near the Lido, far up, on the right hand, as you turn your back to Venice, and I made him put me ashore. I wanted to walk, to move, to shed some of my bewilderment. I crossed the narrow strip and got to the sea-beach—I took my way toward Malamocco. But presently I flung myself down again on the warm sand, in the breeze, on the coarse dry grass. It took it out of me to think I had been so much at fault, that I had unwittingly, but none the less deplorably trifled. But I hadn't given her cause—distinctly I hadn't. I had said to Mrs. Prest that I would make love to her; but it had been a joke without consequences and I had never said it to my victim. I had been as kind as possible because I really liked her; but since when had that become a crime where a woman of such an age and such an appearance was concerned? I am far from remembering clearly the succession of events and feelings during this long day of confusion, which I spent entirely in wandering about, without going home, until late at night: it only comes back to me that there were moments when I pacified my conscience and others when I lashed it into pain. I didn't laugh all day—that I do recollect; the case, however, it might have struck others, seemed to me so little amusing. I should have been better employed perhaps in taking in the comic side of it. At any rate, whether I had given cause or not, there was no doubt whatever that I couldn't pay the price. I couldn't accept the proposal. I couldn't, for a bundle of tattered papers, marry a ridiculous pathetic provincial old woman. It was a proof of how little she supposed the idea would come to me that she should have decided to suggest it herself in that practical argumentative heroic way—with the timidity, however, so much more striking than the boldness, that her reasons appeared to come first and her feelings afterward.

As the day went on I grew to wish I had never heard of Aspern's relics, and I cursed the extravagant curiosity that had put John

Cumnor on the scent of them. We had more than enough material without them, and my predicament was the just punishment of that most fatal of human follies, our not having known when to stop. It was very well to say it was no predicament, but the way out was simple, that I had only to leave Venice by the first train in the morning, after addressing Miss Tina a note which should be placed in her hand as soon as I got clear of the house; for it was strong proof of my quandary that when I tried to make up the note to my taste in advance—I would put it on paper as soon as I got home, before going to bed—I couldn't think of anything but "How can I thank you for the rare confidence you've placed in me?" That would never do; it sounded exactly as if an acceptance were to follow. Of course I might get off without writing at all, but that would be brutal, and my idea was still to exclude brutal solutions. As my confusion cooled I lost myself in wonder at the importance I had attached to Juliana's crumpled scraps; the thought of them became odious to me and I was as vexed with the old witch for the superstition that had prevented her from destroying them as I was with myself for having already spent more money than I could afford in attempting to control their fate. I forget what I did, where I went after leaving the Lido and at what hour or with what recovery of composure I made my way back to my boat. I only know that in the afternoon, when the air was aglow with the sunset, I was standing before the church of Saints John and Paul and looking up at the small square-jawed face of Bartolomeo Colleoni, the terrible *condottiere* who sits so sturdily astride of his huge bronze horse on the high pedestal on which Venetian gratitude maintains him. The statue is incomparable, the finest of all mounted figures, unless that of Marcus Aurelius, who rides benignant before the Roman Capitol, be finer: but I was not thinking of that; I only found myself staring at the triumphant captain as if he had had an oracle on his lips. The western light shines into all his grimness at that hour and makes it wonderfully personal. But he continued to look far over my head, at the red immersion of another day—he had seen so many go down into the lagoon through the centuries—and if he were thinking of battles and stratagems they were of a different quality from any I had to tell him of. He couldn't direct

me what to do, gaze up at him as I might. Was it before this or
after that I wandered about for an hour in the small canals, to the
continued stupefaction of my gondolier, who had never seen me
so restless and yet so void of purpose and could extract from me
no order but "Go anywhere—everywhere—all over the place"? He
reminded me that I had not lunched, and expressed therefore
respectfully the hope that I would dine earlier. He had had long
periods of leisure during the day, when I had left the boat and
rambled, so that I was not obliged to consider him, and I told him
that till the morrow, for reasons, I should touch no meat. It was an
effect of poor Miss Tina's proposal, not altogether auspicious, that
I had quite lost my appetite. I don't know why it happened that on
this occasion I was more than ever struck with that queer air of
sociability, of cousinship and family life, which makes up half the
expression of Venice. Without streets and vehicles, the uproar of
wheels, the brutality of horses, and with its little winding ways
where people crowd together, where voices sound as in the cor-
ridors of a house, where the human step circulates as if it skirted
the angles of furniture and shoes never wear out, the place has the
character of an immense collective apartment, in which Piazza San
Marco is the most ornamented corner, and palaces and churches,
for the rest, play the part of great divans of repose, tables of entertainment, expanses of decoration. And somehow the splendid
common domicile, familiar, domestic and resonant, also resembles
a theatre with its actors clicking over bridges and, in straggling
processions, tripping along fondamentas. As you sit in your
gondola the footways that in certain parts edge the canals assume
to the eye the importance of a stage, meeting it at the same angle,
and the Venetian figures, moving to and fro against the battered
scenery of their little houses of comedy, strike you as members of
an endless dramatic troupe.

I went to bed that night very tired and without being able to
compose an address to Miss Tina. Was this failure the reason why
I became conscious the next morning as soon as I awoke of a deter-
mination to see the poor lady again the first moment she would
receive me? That had something to do with it, but what had still
more was the fact that during my sleep the oddest revulsion had

taken place in my spirit. I found myself aware of this almost as soon as I opened my eyes: it made me jump out of my bed with the movement of a man who remembers that he has left the house-door ajar or a candle burning under a shelf. Was I still in time to save my goods? That question was in my heart; for what had now come to pass was that in the unconscious cerebration of sleep I had swung back to a passionate appreciation of Juliana's treasure. The pieces composing it were now more precious than ever and a positive ferocity had come into my need to acquire them. The condition Miss Tina had attached to that act no longer appeared an obstacle worth thinking of, and for an hour this morning my repentant imagination brushed it aside. It was absurd I should be able to invent nothing; absurd to renounce so easily and turn away helpless from the idea that the only way to become possessed was to unite myself to her for life. I might unite myself, yet I might still have what she had. I must add that by the time I sent down to ask if she would see me I had invented no alternative, though in fact I drew out my dressing in the interest of my wit. This failure was humiliating, yet what could the alternative be? Miss Tina sent back word I might come; and as I descended the stairs and crossed the *sala* to her door—this time she received me in her aunt's forlorn parlour—I hoped she wouldn't think my announcement was to be "favourable". She certainly would have understood my recoil of the day before.

As soon as I came into the room I saw that she had done so, but I also saw something which had not been in my forecast. Poor Miss Tina's sense of her failure had produced a rare alteration in her, but I had been too full of stratagems and spoils to think of that. Now I took it in; I can scarcely tell how it startled me. She stood in the middle of the room with a face of mildness bent upon me, and her look of forgiveness, of absolution, made her angelic. It beautified her; she was younger; she was not a ridiculous old woman. This trick of her expression, this magic of her spirit, transfigured her, and while I still noted it I heard a whisper somewhere in the depths of my conscience: "Why not, after all—why not?" It seemed to me I *could* pay the price. Still more distinctly, however, than the whisper I heard Miss Tina's own voice. I was so struck with the different effect she made on me that at first I wasn't clearly aware of what she was saying; then I recognised she had bade me good-bye—she said something about hoping I should be very happy.

"Good-bye—good-bye?" I repeated with an inflexion interrogative and probably foolish.

I saw she didn't feel the interrogation, she only heard the words: she had strung herself up to accepting our separation and they fell upon her ear as a proof. "Are you going to-day?" she asked. "But it doesn't matter, for whenever you go I shall not see you again. I don't want to." And she smiled strangely, with an infinite gentleness. She had never doubted my having left her the day before in horror. How *could* she, since I hadn't come back before night to contradict, even as a simple form, even as an act of common humanity, such an idea? And now she had the force of soul—Miss Tina with force of soul was a new conception—to smile at me in her abjection.

"What shall you do—where shall you go?" I asked.

"Oh, I don't know. I've done the great thing. I've destroyed the papers."

"Destroyed them?" I wailed.

"Yes; what was I to keep them for? I burnt them last night, one by one, in the kitchen."

"One by one?" I coldly echoed it.

"It took a long time—there were so many." The room seemed to go round me as she said this and a real darkness for a moment descended on my eyes. When it passed Miss Tina was there still, but the transfiguration was over and she had changed back to a plain dingy elderly person. It was in this character she spoke as she said, "I can't stay with you longer, I can't"; and it was in this character she turned her back upon me, as I had turned mine upon her twenty-four hours before, and moved to the door of her room. Here she did what I hadn't done when I quitted her—she paused long enough to give me one look. I have never forgotten it, and I sometimes still suffer from it, though it was not resentful. No, there was no resentment, nothing hard or vindictive in poor Miss Tina; for when, later, I sent her, as the price of the portrait of Jeffrey Aspern, a larger sum of money than I had hoped to be able to

gather for her, writing to her that I had sold the picture, she kept it
with thanks; she never sent it back. I wrote her that I had sold the
picture, but I admitted to Mrs. Prest at the time—I met this other
friend in London that autumn—that it hangs above my writing-
table. When I look at it I can scarcely bear my loss—I mean of the
precious papers.

The Diary of
a Man of Fifty

FLORENCE, *April 5th, 1874.*—They told me I should find Italy greatly changed; and in seven and twenty years there is room for changes. But to me everything is so perfectly the same that I seem to be living my youth over again; all the forgotten impressions of that enchanting time come back to me. At the moment they were powerful enough; but they afterwards faded away. What in the world became of them? What ever becomes of such things, in the long intervals of consciousness? Where do they hide themselves away? in what unvisited cupboards and crannies of our being do they preserve themselves? They are like the lines of a letter written in sympathetic ink; hold the letter to the fire for a while and the grateful warmth brings out the invisible words. It is the warmth of this yellow sun of Florence that has been restoring the text of my own young romance; the thing has been lying before me to-day as a clear, fresh page. There have been moments during the last ten years when I have felt so portentously old, so fagged and finished, that I should have taken as a very bad joke any intimation that this present sense of juvenility was still in store for me. It won't last, at any rate; so I had better make the best of it. But I confess it surprises me. I have led too serious a life; but that perhaps, after all, preserves one's youth. At all events, I have travelled too far, I have worked too hard, I have lived in brutal climates and associated with tiresome people. When a man has reached his fifty-second year without being, materially, the worse for wear—when he has fair health, a fair fortune, a tidy conscience and a complete exemption from embarrassing relatives—I suppose he is bound, in delicacy, to write himself happy. But I confess I shirk this obligation. I have not been miserable; I won't go so far as to say that—or at least as to write it. But happiness—positive happiness—would have been something different. I don't know that it would have been better, by all measurements—that it would have left me better off at the present time. But it certainly would have made this difference—that I should not have been reduced, in pursuit of pleasant images, to disinter a buried episode of more than a quarter of a century ago. I should have found entertainment more—what shall I call it?—more contemporaneous. I should have had a wife and children, and I should not be in the way of making, as the French say, infidelities to the present. Of course it's a great gain to have had an escape, not to have committed an act of thumping folly; and I suppose that, whatever serious step one might have taken at twenty-five, after a struggle, and with a violent effort, and however one's conduct might appear to be justified by events, there would always remain a certain element of regret; a certain sense of loss lurking in the sense of gain; a tendency to wonder, rather wishfully, what *might* have been. What might have been, in this case, would, without doubt, have been very sad, and what has been has been very cheerful and comfortable; but there are nevertheless two or three questions I might ask myself. Why, for instance, have I never married—why have I never been able to care for any woman as I cared for that one? Ah, why are the mountains blue and why is the sunshine warm? Happiness mitigated by impertinent conjectures—that's about my ticket.

6th.—I knew it wouldn't last; it's already passing away. But I have spent a delightful day; I have been strolling all over the place. Everything reminds me of something else, and yet of itself at the same time; my imagination makes a great circuit and comes back to the starting-point. There is that well-remembered odour of spring in the air, and the flowers, as they used to be, are gathered into great sheaves and stacks, all along the rugged base of the Strozzi Palace. I wandered for an hour in the Boboli Gardens; we went there several times together. I remember all those days individually; they seem to me as yesterday. I found the corner where she always chose to sit—the bench of sun-warmed marble, in front of the screen of ilex, with that exuberant statue of Pomona just beside it. The place is exactly the same, except that poor Pomona has lost one of her tapering fingers. I sat there for half-an-hour, and it was strange how near to me she seemed. The place was perfectly empty—that is, it was filled with *her*. I closed my eyes and listened; I could almost hear the rustle of her dress on the gravel. Why do we make such an ado about death? What is it after all but a sort of refinement of life? She died ten years ago, and yet, as I sat there in the sunny stillness, she was a palpable, audible presence. I went afterwards into the gallery of the palace, and wandered for an hour from room to room. The same great pictures hung in the same places and the same dark frescoes arched above them. Twice, of old, I went there with her; she had a great understanding of art. She understood all sorts of things. Before the Madonna of the Chair I stood a long time. The face is not a particle like hers, and yet it reminded me of her. But everything does that. We stood and looked at it together once for half-an-hour; I remember perfectly what she said.

8th.—Yesterday I felt blue—blue and bored; and when I got up this morning I had half a mind to leave Florence. But I went out into the street, beside the Arno, and looked up and down—looked at the yellow river and the violet hills, and then decided to remain—or rather, I decided nothing. I simply stood gazing at the beauty of Florence, and before I had gazed my fill I was in good-humour again, and it was too late to start for Rome. I strolled along the quay, where something presently happened that rewarded me for staying. I stopped in front of a little jeweller's shop, where a great many objects in mosaic were exposed in the window; I stood there for some minutes—I don't know why, for I have no taste for mosaic. In a moment a little girl came and stood beside me—a little girl with a frowsy Italian head, carrying a basket. I turned away, but, as I turned, my eyes happened to fall on her basket. It was covered with a napkin, and on the napkin was pinned a piece of paper, inscribed with an address. This address caught my glance—there was a name on it I knew. It was very legibly written—evidently by a scribe who had made up in zeal what was lacking in skill. *Contessa Salvi-Scarabelli, Via Ghibellina*—so ran the superscription; I looked at it for some moments; it caused me a sudden emotion. Presently the little girl, becoming aware of my attention, glanced up at me, wondering, with a pair of timid brown eyes.

"Are you carrying your basket to the Countess Salvi?" I asked.

The child stared at me. "To the Countess Scarabelli."

"Do you know the Countess?"

"Know her?" murmured the child, with an air of small dismay.

"I mean, have you seen her?"

"Yes, I have seen her." And then, in a moment, with a sudden soft smile—"*E bella!* " said the little girl. She was beautiful herself as she said it.

"Precisely; and is she fair or dark?"

The child kept gazing at me. "*Bionda—bionda*," she answered, looking about into the golden sunshine for a comparison.

"And is she young?"

"She is not young—like me. But she is not old like—like—"

"Like me, eh? And is she married?"

The little girl began to look wise. "I have never seen the Signor Conte."

"And she lives in Via Ghibellina?"

"*Sicuro*. In a beautiful palace."

I had one more question to ask, and I pointed it with certain copper coins. "Tell me a little—is she good?"

The child inspected a moment the contents of her little brown fist. "It's you who are good," she answered.

"Ah, but the Countess?" I repeated.

My informant lowered her big brown eyes, with an air of conscientious meditation that was inexpressibly quaint. "To me she appears so," she said at last, looking up.

"Ah, then she must be so," I said, "because, for your age, you are very intelligent." And having delivered myself of this compliment I walked away and left the little girl counting her *soldi*.

I walked back to the hotel, wondering how I could learn something about the Contessa Salvi-Scarabelli. In the doorway I found the innkeeper, and near him stood a young man whom I immediately perceived to be a compatriot and with whom, apparently, he had been in conversation.

"I wonder whether you can give me a piece of information," I said to the landlord. "Do you know anything about the Count Salvi-Scarabelli?"

The landlord looked down at his boots, then slowly raised his shoulders, with a melancholy smile. "I have many regrets, dear sir——"

"You don't know the name?"

"I know the name, assuredly. But I don't know the gentleman."

I saw that my question had attracted the attention of the young Englishman, who looked at me with a good deal of earnestness. He was apparently satisfied with what he saw, for he presently decided to speak.

"The Count Scarabelli is dead," he said, very gravely.

I looked at him a moment; he was a pleasing young fellow. "And his widow lives," I observed, "in Via Ghibellina?"

"I daresay that is the name of the street." He was a handsome young Englishman, but he was also an awkward one; he wondered who I was and what I wanted, and he did me the honour to perceive that, as regards these points, my appearance was reassuring. But he hesitated, very properly, to talk with a perfect stranger about a lady whom he knew, and he had not the art to conceal his hesitation. I instantly felt it to be singular that though he regarded me as a perfect stranger, I had not the same feeling about him. Whether it was that I had seen him before, or simply that I was struck with his agreeable young face—at any rate, I felt myself as they say here, in sympathy with him. If I have seen him before I don't remember the occasion, and neither, apparently, does he; I suppose it's only a part of the feeling I have had the last three days about everything. It was this feeling that made me suddenly act as if I had known him a long time.

"Do you know the Countess Salvi?" I asked.

He looked at me a little, and then, without resenting the freedom of my question—"The Countess Scarabelli you mean," he said.

"Yes," I answered; "she's the daughter."

"The daughter is a little girl."

"She must be grown up now. She must be—let me see—close upon thirty."

My young Englishman began to smile. "Of whom are you speaking?"

"I was speaking of the daughter," I said, understanding his smile. "But I was thinking of the mother."

"Of the mother?"

"Of a person I knew twenty-seven years ago—the most charming woman I have ever known. She was the Countess Salvi—she lived in a wonderful old house in Via Ghibellina."

"A wonderful old house!" my young Englishman repeated.

"She had a little girl," I went on; "and the little girl was very fair, like her mother; and the mother and daughter had the same name—Bianca." I stopped and looked at my companion, and he blushed a little. "And Bianca Salvi," I continued, "was the most charming woman in the world." He blushed a little more, and I laid my hand on his shoulder. "Do you know why I tell you this? Because you remind me of what I was when I knew her—when I loved her." My poor young Englishman gazed at me with a sort of embarrassed and fascinated stare, and still I went on. "I say that's the reason I told you this—but you'll think it a strange reason. You remind me of my younger self. You needn't resent that—I was a charming young fellow. The Countess Salvi thought so. Her daughter thinks the same of you."

Instantly, instinctively he raised his hand to my arm. "Truly?"

"Ah, you are wonderfully like me!" I said, laughing. "That was just my state of mind. I wanted tremendously to please her." He dropped his hand and looked away, smiling, but with an air of ingenuous confusion which quickened my interest in him. "You don't know what to make of me," I pursued. "You don't know why a stranger should suddenly address you in this way and pretend to read your thoughts. Doubtless you think me a little cracked. Perhaps I am eccentric; but it's not so bad as that. I have lived about the world a great deal, following my profession, which is that of a soldier. I have been in India, in Africa, in Canada, and I have lived a good deal alone. That inclines people, I think, to sudden bursts of confidence. A week ago I came into Italy, where I spent six months when I was your age. I came straight to Florence—I was eager to see it again, on account of associations. They have been crowding upon me ever so thickly. I have taken the liberty of giving you a hint of them." The young man inclined himself a little, in silence, as if he had been struck with a sudden respect. He stood and looked away for a moment at the river and the mountains. "It's very beautiful," I said.

"Oh, it's enchanting," he murmured.

"That's the way I used to talk. But that's nothing to you."

He glanced at me again. "On the contrary, I like to hear."

"Well, then, let us take a walk. If you too are staying at this inn, we are fellow-travellers. We will walk down the Arno to the Cascine. There are several things I should like to ask of you."

My young Englishman assented with an air of almost filial confidence, and we strolled for an hour beside the river and through the shady alleys of that lovely wilderness. We had a great deal of talk: it's not only myself, it's my whole situation over again.

"Are you very fond of Italy?" I asked.

He hesitated a moment. "One can't express that."

"Just so; I couldn't express it. I used to try—I used to write verses. On the subject of Italy I was very ridiculous."

"So am I ridiculous," said my companion.

"No, my dear boy," I answered, "we are not ridiculous; we are two very reasonable, superior people."

"The first time one comes—as I have done—it's a revelation."

"Oh, I remember well; one never forgets it. It's an introduction to beauty."

"And it must be a great pleasure," said my young friend, "to come back."

"Yes, fortunately the beauty is always here. What form of it," I asked, "do you prefer?"

My companion looked a little mystified; and at last he said, "I am very fond of the pictures."

"So was I. And among the pictures, which do you like best?"

"Oh, a great many."

"So did I; but I had certain favourites."

Again the young man hesitated a little, and then he confessed that the group of painters he preferred on the whole to all others was that of the early Florentines.

I was so struck with this that I stopped short. "That was exactly my taste!" And then I passed my hand into his arm and we went our way again.

We sat down on an old stone bench in the Cascine, and a solemn blank-eyed Hermes, with wrinkles accentuated by the dust of ages, stood above us and listened to our talk.

"The Countess Salvi died ten years ago," I said.

My companion admitted that he had heard her daughter say so.

"After I knew her she married again," I added. "The Count Salvi died before I knew her—a couple of years after their marriage."

"Yes, I have heard that."

"And what else have you heard?"

My companion stared at me; he had evidently heard nothing.

"She was a very interesting woman—there are a great many things to be said about her. Later, perhaps, I will tell you. Has the daughter the same charm?"

"You forget," said my young man, smiling, "that I have never seen the mother."

"Very true. I keep confounding. But the daughter—how long have you known her?"

"Only since I have been here. A very short time."

"A week?"

For a moment he said nothing. "A month."

"That's just the answer I should have made. A week, a month—it was all the same to me."

"I think it is more than a month," said the young man.

"It's probably six. How did you make her acquaintance?"

"By a letter—an introduction given me by a friend in England."

"The analogy is complete," I said. "But the friend who gave me my letter to Madame de Salvi died many years ago. He, too, admired her greatly. I don't know why it never came into my mind that her daughter might be living in Florence. Somehow I took for granted it was all over. I never thought of the little girl; I never heard what had become of her. I walked past the palace yesterday and saw that it was occupied; but I took for granted it had changed hands."

"The Countess Scarabelli," said my friend, "brought it to her husband as her marriage-portion."

"I hope he appreciated it! There is a fountain in the court, and there is a charming old garden beyond it. The Countess's sitting-room looks into that garden. The staircase is of white marble, and there is a medallion by Luca della Robbia set into the wall at the place where it makes a bend. Before you come into the drawing-room you stand a moment in a great vaulted place hung round with faded tapestry, paved with bare tiles, and furnished only with three chairs. In the drawing-room, above the fire-place, is a superb Andrea del Sarto. The furniture is covered with pale sea-green."

My companion listened to all this.

"The Andrea del Sarto is there; it's magnificent. But the furniture is in pale red."

"Ah, they have changed it then—in twenty-seven years."

"And there's a portrait of Madame de Salvi," continued my friend.

I was silent a moment. "I should like to see that."

He too was silent. Then he asked, "Why don't you go and see it? If you knew the mother so well, why don't you call upon the daughter?"

"From what you tell me I am afraid."

"What have I told you to make you afraid?"

I looked a little at his ingenuous countenance. "The mother was a very dangerous woman."

The young Englishman began to blush again. "The daughter is not," he said.

"Are you very sure?"

He didn't say he was sure, but he presently inquired in what way the Countess Salvi had been dangerous.

"You must not ask me that," I answered; "for, after all, I desire to remember only what was good in her." And as we walked back I begged him to render me the service of mentioning my name to his friend, and of saying that I had known her mother well and that I asked permission to come and see her.

9th.—I have seen that poor boy half-a-dozen times again, and a most amiable young fellow he is. He continues to represent to me, in the most extraordinary manner, my own young identity; the correspondence is perfect at all points, save that he is a better boy than I. He is evidently acutely interested in his Countess, and leads quite the same life with her that I led with Madame de Salvi. He goes to see her every evening and stays half the night; these Florentines keep the most extraordinary hours. I remember, towards 3 A.M., Madame de Salvi used to turn me out. "Come, come," she would say, "it's time to go. If you were to stay later people might talk." I don't know at what time he comes home, but I suppose his evening seems as short as mine did. To-day he brought me a message from his Contessa—a very gracious little speech. She remembered often to have heard her mother speak of me—she called me her English friend. All her mother's friends were dear to her, and she begged I would do her the honour to come and see her. She is always at home of an evening. Poor young Stanmer (he is of the Devonshire Stanmers—a great property) reported this speech verbatim, and of course it can't in the least signify to him that a poor grizzled, battered soldier, old enough to be his father, should come to call upon his *inammorata*. But I remember how it used to matter to me when other men came; that's a point of difference. However, it's only because I'm so old. At twenty-five I shouldn't have been afraid of myself at fifty-two. Camerino was thirty-four—and then the others! She was always at home in the evening, and they all used to come. They were old Florentine names. But she used to let me stay after them all; she thought an old English name as good. What a transcendent coquette!... But *basta così*, as she used to say. I meant to go to-night to Casa Salvi, but I couldn't bring myself to the point. I don't know what I'm afraid of; I used to be in a hurry enough to go there once. I suppose I am afraid of the very look of the place—of the old rooms, the old walls. I shall go to-morrow night. I am afraid of the very echoes.

10th.—She has the most extraordinary resemblance to her mother. When I went in I was tremendously startled; I stood staring at her. I have just come home; it is past midnight; I have been all the evening at Casa Salvi. It is very warm—my window is open—I can look out on the river, gliding past in the starlight. So, of old, when I came home, I used to stand and look out. There are the same cypresses on the opposite hills.

Poor young Stanmer was there, and three or four other admirers; they all got up when I came in. I think I had been talked about, and there was some curiosity. But why should I have been talked about? They were all youngish men—none of them of my time. She is a wonderful likeness of her mother; I couldn't get over it. Beautiful like her mother, and yet with the same faults in her face; but with her mother's perfect head and brow and sympathetic, almost pitying eyes. Her face has just that peculiarity of her mother's, which, of all human countenances that I have ever known, was the one that passed most quickly and completely from the expression of gaiety to that of repose. Repose, in her face, always suggested sadness; and while you were watching it with a kind of awe, and wondering of what tragic secret it was the token, it kindled, on the instant, into a radiant Italian smile. The Countess Scarabelli's smiles to-night, however, were almost uninterrupted. She greeted me—divinely, as her mother used to do; and young Stanmer sat in the corner of the sofa—as I used to do—and watched her while she talked. She is thin and very fair, and was dressed in light, vaporous black: that completes the resemblance. The house, the rooms, are almost absolutely the same; there may be changes of detail, but they don't modify the general effect. There are the same precious pictures on the walls of the salon—the same great dusky fresco in the concave ceiling. The daughter is not rich, I suppose, any more than the mother. The furniture is worn and faded, and I was admitted by a solitary servant who carried a twinkling taper before me up the great dark marble staircase.

"I have often heard of you," said the Countess, as I sat down near her; "my mother often spoke of you."

"Often?" I answered. "I am surprised at that."

"Why are you surprised? Were you not good friends?"

"Yes, for a certain time—very good friends. But I was sure she had forgotten me."

"She never forgot," said the Countess, looking at me intently and smiling. "She was not like that."

"She was not like most other women in any way," I declared.

"Ah, she was charming," cried the Countess, rattling open her fan. "I have always been very curious to see you. I have received an impression of you."

"A good one, I hope."

She looked at me, laughing, and not answering this: it was just her mother's trick.

" 'My Englishman,' she used to call you—'*il mio Inglese*.' "

"I hope she spoke of me kindly," I insisted.

The Countess, still laughing, gave a little shrug, balancing her hand to and fro. "So-so; I always supposed you had had a quarrel. You don't mind my being frank like this—eh?"

"I delight in it; it reminds me of your mother."

"Every one tells me that. But I am not clever like her. You will see for yourself."

"That speech," I said, "completes the resemblance. She was always pretending she was not clever, and in reality——"

"In reality she was an angel, eh? To escape from dangerous comparisons I will admit then that I am clever. That will make a difference. But let us talk of you. You are very—how shall I say it?—very eccentric."

"Is that what your mother told you?"

"To tell the truth, she spoke of you as a great original. But aren't all Englishmen eccentric? All except that one!" and the Countess pointed to poor Stanmer, in his corner of the sofa.

"Oh, I know just what he is," I said.

"He's as quiet as a lamb—he's like all the world," cried the Countess.

"Like all the world—yes. He is in love with you."

She looked at me with sudden gravity. "I don't object to your saying that for all the world—but I do for him."

"Well," I went on, "he is peculiar in this: he is rather afraid of you."

Instantly she began to smile; she turned her face toward Stanmer. He had seen that we were talking about him; he coloured and got up—then came toward us.

"I like men who are afraid of nothing," said our hostess.

"I know what you want," I said to Stanmer. "You want to know what the Signora Contessa says about you."

Stanmer looked straight into her face, very gravely. "I don't care a straw what she says."

"You are almost a match for the Signora Contessa," I answered. "She declares she doesn't care a pin's head what you think."

"I recognise the Countess's style!" Stanmer exclaimed, turning away.

"One would think," said the Countess, "that you were trying to make a quarrel between us."

I watched him move away to another part of the great saloon; he stood in front of the Andrea del Sarto, looking up at it. But he was not seeing it; he was listening to what we might say. I often stood there in just that way. "He can't quarrel with you, any more than I could have quarrelled with your mother."

"Ah, but you did. Something painful passed between you."

"Yes, it was painful, but it was not a quarrel. I went away one day and never saw her again. That was all."

The Countess looked at me gravely. "What do you call it when a man does that?"

"It depends upon the case."

"Sometimes," said the Countess in French, "it's a *lâcheté*."

"Yes, and sometimes, it's an act of wisdom."

"And sometimes," rejoined the Countess, "it's a mistake."

I shook my head. "For me it was no mistake."

She began to laugh again. "Caro Signore, you're a great original. What had my poor mother done to you?"

I looked at our young Englishman, who still had his back turned to us and was staring up at the picture. "I will tell you some other time," I said.

"I shall certainly remind you; I am very curious to know." Then she opened and shut her fan two or three times, still looking at me. What eyes they have! "Tell me a little," she went on, "if I may ask without indiscretion. Are you married?"

"No, Signora Contessa."

"Isn't that at least a mistake?"

"Do I look very unhappy?"

She dropped her head a little to one side. "For an Englishman—no!"

"Ah," said I, laughing, "you are quite as clever as your mother."

"And they tell me that you are a great soldier," she continued; "you have lived in India. It was very kind of you, so far away, to have remembered our poor dear Italy."

"One always remembers Italy; the distance makes no difference. I remembered it well the day I heard of your mother's death!"

"Ah, that was a sorrow!" said the Countess. "There's not a day that I don't weep for her. But *che vuole*? She's a saint in paradise."

"*Sicuro*," I answered; and I looked some time at the ground. "But tell me about yourself, dear lady," I asked at last, raising my eyes. "You have also had the sorrow of losing your husband."

"I am a poor widow, as you see. *Che vuole?* My husband died after three years of marriage."

I waited for her to remark that the late Count Scarabelli was also a saint in paradise, but I waited in vain.

"That was like your distinguished father," I said.

"Yes, he too died young. I can't be said to have known him; I was but of the age of my own little girl. But I weep for him all the more."

Again I was silent for a moment.

"It was in India too," I said presently, "that I heard of your mother's second marriage."

The Countess raised her eyebrows.

"In India, then, one hears of everything! Did that news please you?"

"Well, since you ask me—no."

"I understand that," said the Countess, looking at her open fan. "I shall not marry again like that."

"That's what your mother said to me," I ventured to observe.

She was not offended, but she rose from her seat and stood looking at me a moment. Then—

"You should not have gone away!" she exclaimed.

I stayed for another hour; it is a very pleasant house. Two or three of the men who were sitting there seemed very civil and intelligent; one of them was a major of engineers, who offered me a profusion of information upon the new organisation of the Italian army. While he talked, however, I was observing our hostess, who was talking with the others; very little, I noticed, with her young Inglese. She is altogether charming—full of frankness and freedom, of that inimitable *disinvoltura* which in an English-woman would be vulgar, and which in her is simply the perfection of apparent spontaneity. But for all her spontaneity she's as subtle as a needlepoint, and knows tremendously well what she is about. If she is not a consummate coquette... What had she in her head when she said that I should not have gone away?—Poor little Stanmer didn't go away. I left him there at midnight.

12th.—I found him to-day sitting in the church of Santa Croce, into which I wandered to escape from the heat of the sun.

In the nave it was cool and dim; he was staring at the blaze of candles on the great altar, and thinking, I am sure, of his in-comparable Countess. I sat down beside him, and after a while, as if to avoid the appearance of eagerness, he asked me how I had enjoyed my visit to Casa Salvi, and what I thought of the *padrona*.

"I think half a dozen things," I said; "but I can only tell you one now. She's an enchantress. You shall hear the rest when we have left the church."

"An enchantress?" repeated Stanmer, looking at me askance.

He is a very simple youth, but who am I to blame him?

"A charmer," I said; "a fascinatress!"

He turned away, staring at the altar-candles.

"An artist—an actress," I went on, rather brutally.

He gave me another glance.

"I think you are telling me all," he said.

"No, no, there is more." And we sat a long time in silence.

At last he proposed that we should go out; and we passed in the street, where the shadows had begun to stretch themselves.

"I don't know what you mean by her being an actress," he said, as we turned homeward.

"I suppose not. Neither should I have known, if any one had said that to me."

"You are thinking about the mother," said Stanmer. "Why are you always bringing *her* in?"

"My dear boy, the analogy is so great; it forces itself upon me."

He stopped, and stood looking at me with his modest,

perplexed young face. I thought he was going to exclaim—"The analogy be hanged!"—but he said after a moment—

"Well, what does it prove?"

"I can't say it proves anything; but it suggests a great many things."

"Be so good as to mention a few," he said, as we walked on.

"You are not sure of her yourself," I began.

"Never mind that—go on with your analogy."

"That's a part of it. You *are* very much in love with her."

"That's a part of it too, I suppose?"

"Yes, as I have told you before. You are in love with her, and yet you can't make her out; that's just where I was with regard to Madame de Salvi."

"And she too was an enchantress, an actress, an artist, and all the rest of it?"

"She was the most perfect coquette I ever knew, and the most dangerous, because the most finished."

"What you mean, then, is that her daughter is a finished coquette?"

"I rather think so."

Stanmer walked along for some moments in silence.

"Seeing that you suppose me to be a—a great admirer of the Countess," he said at last, "I am rather surprised at the freedom with which you speak of her."

I confessed that I was surprised at it myself. "But it's on account of the interest I take in you."

"I am immensely obliged to you!" said the poor boy.

"Ah, of course you don't like it. That is, you like my interest—I don't see how you can help liking that; but you don't like my freedom. That's natural enough; but, my dear young friend, I want only to help you. If a man had said to me—so many years ago— what I am saying to you, I should certainly also, at first, have thought him a great brute. But, after a little, I should have been grateful—I should have felt that he was helping me."

"You seem to have been very well able to help yourself," said Stanmer. "You tell me you made your escape."

"Yes, but it was at the cost of infinite perplexity—of what I may call keen suffering. I should like to save you all that."

"I can only repeat—it is really very kind of you."

"Don't repeat it too often, or I shall begin to think you don't mean it."

"Well," said Stanmer, "I think this, at any rate—that you take an extraordinary responsibility in trying to put a man out of conceit of a woman who, as he believes, may make him very happy."

I grasped his arm, and we stopped, going on with our talk like a couple of Florentines.

"Do you wish to marry her?"

He looked away, without meeting my eyes. "It's a great responsibility," he repeated.

"Before Heaven," I said, "I would have married the mother! You are exactly in my situation."

"Don't you think you rather overdo the analogy?" asked poor Stanmer.

"A little more, a little less—it doesn't matter. I believe you are in my shoes. But of course if you prefer it I will beg a thousand pardons and leave them to carry you where they will."

He had been looking away, but now he slowly turned his face and met my eyes. "You have gone too far to retreat; what is it you know about her?"

"About this one—nothing. But about the other——"

"I care nothing about the other!"

"My dear fellow," I said, "they are mother and daughter—they are as like as two of Andrea's Madonnas."

"If they resemble each other, then, you were simply mistaken in the mother."

I took his arm and we walked on again; there seemed no adequate reply to such a charge. "Your state of mind brings back my own so completely," I said presently. "You admire her—you adore her, and yet, secretly, you mistrust her. You are enchanted with her personal charm, her grace, her wit, her everything; and yet in your private heart you are afraid of her."

"Afraid of her?"

"Your mistrust keeps rising to the surface; you can't rid yourself of the suspicion that at the bottom of all things she is hard and cruel, and you would be immensely relieved if some one should persuade you that your suspicion is right."

Stanmer made no direct reply to this; but before we reached the hotel he said—"What did you ever know about the mother?"

"It's a terrible story," I answered.

He looked at me askance. "What did she do?"

"Come to my rooms this evening and I will tell you."

He declared he would, but he never came. Exactly the way I should have acted!

14th.—I went again, last evening, to Casa Salvi, where I found the same little circle, with the addition of a couple of ladies. Stanmer was there, trying hard to talk to one of them, but making, I am sure, a very poor business of it. The Countess—well, the Countess was admirable. She greeted me like a friend of ten years, toward whom familiarity should not have engendered a want of ceremony; she made me sit near her, and she asked me a dozen questions about my health and my occupations.

"I live in the past," I said. "I go into the galleries, into the old palaces and the churches. To-day I spent an hour in Michael Angelo's chapel, at San Lorenzo."

"Ah, yes, that's the past," said the Countess. "Those things are very old."

"Twenty-seven years old," I answered.

"Twenty-seven? *Altro!* "

"I mean my own past," I said. "I went to a great many of those places with your mother."

"Ah, the pictures are beautiful," murmured the Countess, glancing at Stanmer.

"Have you lately looked at any of them?" I asked. "Have you gone to the galleries with *him*?"

She hesitated a moment, smiling. "It seems to me that your question is a little impertinent. But I think you are like that."

"A little impertinent? Never. As I say, your mother did me the honour, more than once, to accompany me to the Uffizzi."

"My mother must have been very kind to you."

"So it seemed to me at the time."

"At the time, only?"

"Well, if you prefer, so it seems to me now."

"Eh," said the Countess, "she made sacrifices."

"To what, cara Signora? She was perfectly free. Your lamented father was dead—and she had not yet contracted her second marriage."

"If she was intending to marry again, it was all the more reason she should have been careful."

I looked at her a moment; she met my eyes gravely, over the top of her fan. "Are *you* very careful?" I said.

She dropped her fan with a certain violence. "Ah, yes, you are impertinent!"

"Ah, no," I said. "Remember that I am old enough to be your father; that I knew you when you were three years old. I may surely ask such questions. But you are right; one must do your mother justice. She was certainly thinking of her second marriage."

"You have not forgiven her that!" said the Countess, very gravely.

"Have you?" I asked, more lightly.

"I don't judge my mother. That is a mortal sin. My stepfather was very kind to me."

"I remember him," I said; "I saw him a great many times—your mother already received him."

My hostess sat with lowered eyes, saying nothing; but she presently looked up.

"She was very unhappy with my father."

"That I can easily believe. And your stepfather—is he still living?"

"He died—before my mother."

"Did he fight any more duels?"

"He was killed in a duel," said the Countess, discreetly.

It seems almost monstrous, especially as I can give no reason for it—but this announcement, instead of shocking me, caused me to feel a strange exhilaration. Most assuredly, after all these years, I bear the poor man no resentment. Of course I controlled my manner, and simply remarked to the Countess that as his fault had been, so was his punishment. I think, however, that the feeling of which I speak was at the bottom of my saying to her that I hoped that, unlike her mother's, her own brief married life had been happy.

"If it was not," she said, "I have forgotten it now."—I wonder if the late Count Scarabelli was also killed in a duel, and if his adversary. . . . Is it on the books that his adversary, as well, shall perish by the pistol? Which of those gentlemen is he, I wonder? Is it reserved for poor little Stanmer to put a bullet into him? No; poor little Stanmer, I trust, will do as I did. And yet, unfortunately for him, that woman is consummately plausible. She was wonderfully nice last evening; she was really irresistible. Such frankness and freedom, and yet something so soft and womanly; such graceful gaiety, so much of the brightness, without any of the stiffness, of good breeding, and over it all something so picturesquely simple and southern. She is a perfect Italian. But she comes honestly by it. After the talk I have just jotted down she changed her place, and the conversation for half-an-hour was general. Stanmer indeed said very little; partly, I suppose, because he is shy of talking a foreign tongue. Was I like that—was I so constantly silent? I suspect I was when I was perplexed, and Heaven knows that very often my perplexity was extreme. Before I went away I had a few more words *tête-à-tête* with the Countess.

"I hope you are not leaving Florence yet," she said; "you will stay a while longer?"

I answered that I came only for a week, and that my week was over.

"I stay on from day to day, I am so much interested."

"Eh, it's the beautiful moment. I'm glad our city pleases you!"

"Florence pleases me—and I take a paternal interest in our young friend," I added, glancing at Stanmer. "I have become very fond of him."

"*Bel tipo inglese,*" said my hostess. "And he is very intelligent; he has a beautiful mind."

She stood there resting her smile and her clear, expressive eyes upon me.

"I don't like to praise him too much," I rejoined, "lest I should appear to praise myself; he reminds me so much of what I was at his age. If your beautiful mother were to come to life for an hour she would see the resemblance."

She gave me a little amused stare.

"And yet you don't look at all like him!"

"Ah, you didn't know me when I was twenty-five. I was very handsome! And, moreover, it isn't that, it's the mental resemblance. I was ingenuous, candid, trusting, like him."

"Trusting? I remember my mother once telling me that you were the most suspicious and jealous of men!"

"I fell into a suspicious mood, but I was, fundamentally, not in the least addicted to thinking evil. I couldn't easily imagine any harm of any one."

"And so you mean that Mr. Stanmer is in a suspicious mood?"

"Well, I mean that his situation is the same as mine."

The Countess gave me one of her serious looks.

"Come," she said, "what was it—this famous situation of yours? I have heard you mention it before."

"Your mother might have told you, since she occasionally did me the honour to speak of me."

"All my mother ever told me was that you were a sad puzzle to her."

At this, of course, I laughed out—I laugh still as I write it.

"Well, then, that was my situation—I was a sad puzzle to a very clever woman."

"And you mean, therefore, that I am a puzzle to poor Mr. Stanmer?"

"He is racking his brains to make you out. Remember it was you who said he was intelligent."

She looked round at him, and as fortune would have it, his appearance at that moment quite confirmed my assertion. He was lounging back in his chair with an air of indolence rather too marked for a drawing-room, and staring at the ceiling with the expression of a man who has just been asked a conundrum. Madame Scarabelli seemed struck with his attitude.

"Don't you see," I said, "he can't read the riddle?"

"You yourself," she answered, "said he was incapable of thinking evil. I should be sorry to have him think any evil of *me*."

And she looked straight at me—seriously, appealingly—with

her beautiful candid brow.

I inclined myself, smiling, in a manner which might have meant—

"How could that be possible?"

"I have a great esteem for him," she went on; "I want him to think well of me. If I am a puzzle to him, do me a little service. Explain me to him."

"Explain you, dear lady?"

"You are older and wiser than he. Make him understand me."

She looked deep into my eyes for a moment, and then she turned away.

26th.—I have written nothing for a good many days, but meanwhile I have been half a dozen times to Casa Salvi. I have seen a good deal also of my young friend—had a good many walks and talks with him. I have proposed to him to come with me to Venice for a fortnight, but he won't listen to the idea of leaving Florence. He is very happy in spite of his doubts, and I confess that in the perception of his happiness I have lived over again my own. This is so much the case that when, the other day, he at last made up his mind to ask me to tell him the wrong that Madame de Salvi had done me, I rather checked his curiosity. I told him that if he was bent upon knowing I would satisfy him, but that it seemed a pity, just now, to indulge in painful imagery.

"But I thought you wanted so much to put me out of conceit of our friend."

"I admit I am inconsistent, but there are various reasons for it. In the first place—it's obvious—I am open to the charge of playing a double game. I profess an admiration for the Countess Scarabelli, for I accept her hospitality, and at the same time I attempt to poison your mind; isn't that the proper expression? I can't exactly make up my mind to that, though my admiration for the Countess and my desire to prevent you from taking a foolish step are equally sincere. And then, in the second place you seem to me on the whole so happy! One hesitates to destroy an illusion, no matter how pernicious, that is so delightful while it lasts. These are the rare moments of life. To be young and ardent, in the midst of an Italian spring, and to believe in the moral perfection of a beautiful woman—what an admirable situation! Float with the current; I'll stand on the brink and watch you."

"Your real reason is that you feel you have no case against the poor lady," said Stanmer. "You admire her as much as I do."

"I just admitted that I admired her. I never said she was a vulgar flirt; her mother was an absolutely scientific one. Heaven knows I admired that! It's a nice point, however, how much one is bound in honour not to warn a young friend against a dangerous woman because one also has relations of civility with the lady."

"In such a case," said Stanmer, "I would break off my relations."

I looked at him, and I think I laughed.

"Are you jealous of me, by chance?"

He shook his head emphatically.

"Not in the least; I like to see you there, because your conduct contradicts your words."

"I have always said that the Countess is fascinating."

"Otherwise," said Stanmer, "in the case you speak of I would give the lady notice."

"Give her notice?"

"Mention to her that you regard her with suspicion, and that you propose to do your best to rescue a simple-minded youth from her wiles. That would be more loyal." And he began to laugh again.

It is not the first time he has laughed at me; but I have never minded it, because I have always understood it.

"Is that what you recommend me to say to the Countess?" I asked.

"Recommend you!" he exclaimed, laughing again; "I recommend nothing. I may be the victim to be rescued, but I am at least not a partner to the conspiracy. Besides," he added in a moment, "the Countess knows your state of mind."

"Has she told you so?"

Stanmer hesitated.

"She has begged me to listen to everything you may say against her. She declares that she has a good conscience."

"Ah," said I, "she's an accomplished woman!"

And it is indeed very clever of her to take that tone. Stanmer afterwards assured me explicitly that he has never given her a hint of the liberties I have taken in conversation with—what shall I call it?—with her moral nature; she has guessed them for herself. She must hate me intensely, and yet her manner has always been so charming to me! She is truly an accomplished woman!

May 4th.—I have stayed away from Casa Salvi for a week, but I have lingered on in Florence, under a mixture of impulses. I have had it on my conscience not to go near the Countess again—and yet from the moment she is aware of the way I feel about her, it is open war. There need be no scruples on either side. She is as free to use every possible art to entangle poor Stanmer more closely as I am to clip her fine-spun meshes. Under the circumstances, however, we naturally shouldn't meet very cordially. But as regards her meshes, why, after all, should I clip them? It would really be very interesting to see Stanmer swallowed up. I should like to see how he would agree with her after she had devoured him—(to what vulgar imagery, by the way, does curiosity reduce a man!) Let him finish the story in his own way, as I finished it in mine. It is the same story; but why, a quarter of a century later, should it have the same *dénoûment*? Let him make his own *dénoûment*.

5th.—Hang it, however, I don't want the poor boy to be miserable.

6th.—Ah, but did my *dénoûment* then prove such a happy one?

7th.—He came to my room late last night; he was much excited.

"What was it she did to you?" he asked.

I answered him first with another question. "Have you quarrelled with the Countess?"

But he only repeated his own. "What was it she did to you?"

"Sit down and I'll tell you." And he sat there beside the candle, staring at me. "There was a man always there—Count Camerino."

"The man she married?"

"The man she married. I was very much in love with her, and yet I didn't trust her. I was sure that she lied; I believed that she could be cruel. Nevertheless, at moments, she had a charm which made it pure pedantry to be conscious of her faults; and while these moments lasted I would have done anything for her. Unfortunately, they didn't last long. But you know what I mean; am I not describing the Scarabelli?"

"The Countess Scarabelli never lied!" cried Stanmer.

"That's just what I would have said to any one who should have made the insinuation! But I suppose you are not asking me the question you put to me just now from dispassionate curiosity."

"A man may want to know!" said the innocent fellow.

I couldn't help laughing out. "This, at any rate, is my story. Camerino was always there; he was a sort of fixture in the house. If I had moments of dislike for the divine Bianca, I had no moments of liking for him. And yet he was a very agreeable fellow, very civil, very intelligent, not in the least disposed to make a quarrel with me. The trouble of course was simply that I was jealous of him. I don't know, however, on what ground I could have quarrelled with him, for I had no definite rights. I can't say what I expected—I can't say what, as the matter stood, I was prepared to do. With my name and my prospects, I might perfectly have offered her my hand. I am not sure that she would have accepted it—I am by no means clear that she wanted that. But she wanted, wanted keenly, to attach me to her; she wanted to have me about. I should have been capable of giving up everything—England, my career, my family—simply to devote myself to her, to live near her and see her every day."

"Why didn't you do it, then?" asked Stanmer.

"Why don't you?"

"To be a proper rejoinder to my question," he said, rather neatly, "yours should be asked twenty-five years hence."

"It remains perfectly true that at a given moment I was capable of doing as I say. That was what she wanted—a rich, susceptible, credulous, convenient young Englishman established near her *en permanence*. And yet," I added, "I must do her complete justice. I honestly believe she was fond of me." At this Stanmer got up and walked to the window; he stood looking out a moment, and then he turned round. "You know she was older than I," I went on. "Madame Scarabelli is older than you. One day in the garden, her mother asked me in an angry tone why I disliked Camerino; for I had been at no pains to conceal my feeling about him, and something had just happened to bring it out. 'I dislike him,' I said, 'because you like him so much.' 'I assure you I don't like him,' she answered. 'He has all the appearance of being your lover,' I retorted. It was a brutal speech, certainly, but any other man in my place would have made it. She took it very strangely; she turned pale, but she was not indignant. 'How can he be my lover after what he has done?' she asked. 'What has he done?' She hesitated a good while, then she said: 'He killed my husband.' 'Good heavens!' I cried, 'and you receive him!' Do you know what she said? She said, '*Che vuole?*'"

"Is that all?" asked Stanmer.

"No; she went on to say that Camerino had killed Count Salvi in a duel, and she admitted that her husband's jealousy had been the occasion of it. The Count, it appeared, was a monster of jealousy—he had led her a dreadful life. He himself, meanwhile, had been anything but irreproachable; he had done a mortal injury to a man of whom he pretended to be a friend, and this affair had become notorious. The gentleman in question had demanded satisfaction for his outraged honour; but for some reason or other (the Countess, to do her justice, did not tell me that her husband was a coward), he had not as yet obtained it. The duel with Camerino had come on first; in an access of jealous fury the Count had struck Camerino in the face; and this outrage, I know not how justly, was deemed expiable before the other. By an extra-ordinary arrangement (the Italians have certainly no sense of fair play), the other man was allowed to be Camerino's second. The duel was fought with swords, and the Count received a wound of which, though at first it was not expected to be fatal, he died on the following day. The matter was hushed up as much as possible for the sake of the Countess's good name, and so successfully that it was presently observed that, among the public, the other gentle-man had the credit of having put his blade through M. de Salvi. This gentleman took a fancy not to contradict the impression, and it was allowed to subsist. So long as *he* consented, it was of course in Camerino's interest not to contradict it, as it left him much more free to keep up his intimacy with the Countess."

Stanmer had listened to all this with extreme attention. "Why didn't *she* contradict it?"

I shrugged my shoulders. "I am bound to believe it was for the same reason. I was horrified, at any rate, by the whole story. I was extremely shocked at the Countess's want of dignity in continuing to see the man by whose hand her husband had fallen."

"The husband had been a great brute, and it was not known," said Stanmer.

"Its not being known made no difference. And as for Salvi having been a brute, that is but a way of saying that his wife, and the man whom his wife subsequently married, didn't like him."

Stanmer hooked extremely meditative; his eyes were fixed on mine. "Yes, that marriage is hard to get over. It was not becoming."

"Ah," said I, "what a long breath I drew when I heard of it! I remember the place and the hour. It was at a hill-station in India, seven years after I had left Florence. The post brought me some English papers, and in one of them was a letter from Italy, with a lot of so-called 'fashionable intelligence.' There, among various scandals in high-life, and other delectable items, I read that the Countess Bianca Salvi, famous for some years as the presiding genius of the most agreeable *salon* in Florence, was about to bestow her hand upon Count Camerino, a distinguished Bo-lognese. Ah, my dear boy, it was a tremendous escape! I had been ready to marry the woman who was capable of that! But my instinct had warned me, and I had trusted my instinct."

" 'Instinct's everything,' as Falstaff says!" And Stanmer began to laugh. "Did you tell Madame de Salvi that your instinct was against her?"

"No; I told her that she frightened me, shocked me, horrified me."

"That's about the same thing. And what did she say?"

"She asked me what I would have? I called her friendship with Camerino a scandal, and she answered that her husband had been a brute. Besides, no one knew it; therefore it was no scandal. Just *your* argument! I retorted that this was odious reasoning, and that she had no moral sense. We had a passionate argument, and I declared I would never see her again. In the heat of my displeasure I left Florence, and I kept my vow. I never saw her again."

"You couldn't have been much in love with her," said Stanmer.

"I was not—three months after."

"If you had been you would have come back—three days after."

"So doubtless it seems to you. All I can say is that it was the great effort of my life. Being a military man, I have had on various occasions to face the enemy. But it was not then I needed my resolution; it was when I left Florence in a postchaise."

Stanmer turned about the room two or three times, and then he said: "I don't understand! I don't understand why she should have told you that Camerino had killed her husband. It could only damage her."

"She was afraid it would damage her more that I should think he was her lover. She wished to say the thing that would most effectually persuade me that he was not her lover—that he could never be. And then she wished to get the credit of being very frank."

"Good heavens, how you must have analysed her!" cried my companion, staring.

"There is nothing so analytic as disillusionment. But there it is. She married Camerino."

"Yes, I don't like that," said Stanmer. He was silent a while, and then he added—"Perhaps she wouldn't have done so if you had remained."

He has a little innocent way! "Very likely she would have dispensed with the ceremony," I answered dryly.

"Upon my word," he said, "you *have* analysed her!"

"You ought to be grateful to me. I have done for you what you seem unable to do for yourself."

"I don't see any Camerino in my case," he said.

"Perhaps among those gentlemen I can find one for you."

"Thank you," he cried; "I'll take care of that myself!" And he went away—satisfied, I hope.

10th.—He's an obstinate little wretch; it irritates me to see him sticking to it. Perhaps he is looking for his Camerino. I shall leave him at any rate to his fate; it is growing insupportably hot.

11th.—I went this evening to bid farewell to the Scarabelli. There was no one there; she was alone in her great dusky drawing-room, which was lighted only by a couple of candles, with the immense windows open over the garden. She was dressed in white; she was deucedly pretty. She asked me of course why I had been so long without coming.

"I think you say that only for form," I answered. "I imagine you know."

"*Chè!* what have I done?"

"Nothing at all. You are too wise for that."

She looked at me a while. "I think you are a little crazy."

"Ah no, I am only too sane. I have too much reason rather than too little."

"You have at any rate what we call a fixed idea."

"There is no harm in that so long as it's a good one."

"But yours is abominable!" she exclaimed with a laugh.

"Of course you can't like me or my ideas. All things considered, you have treated me with wonderful kindness, and I thank you and kiss your hands. I leave Florence to-morrow."

"I won't say I'm sorry!" she said, laughing again. "But I am very glad to have seen you. I always wondered about you. You are a curiosity."

"Yes, you must find me so. A man who can resist your charms! The fact is, I can't. This evening you are enchanting; and it is the first time I have been alone with you."

She gave no heed to this; she turned away. But in a moment she came back, and stood looking at me, and her beautiful solemn eyes seemed to shine in the dimness of the room.

"How *could* you treat my mother so?" she asked.

"Treat her so?"

"How could you desert the most charming woman in the world?"

"It was not a case of desertion; and if it had been it seems to me she was consoled."

At this moment there was the sound of a step in the ante-chamber, and I saw that the Countess perceived it to be Stanmer's.

"That wouldn't have happened," she murmured. "My poor mother needed a protector."

Stanmer came in, interrupting our talk, and looking at me, I thought, with a little air of bravado. He must think me indeed a tiresome, meddlesome bore; and upon my word, turning it all over, I wonder at his docility. After all, he's five-and-twenty—and yet, I *must* add, it *does* irritate me—the way he sticks! He was followed in a moment by two or three of the regular Italians, and I made my visit short.

"Good-bye, Countess," I said; and she gave me her hand in silence. "Do *you* need a protector?" I added, softly.

She looked at me from head to foot, and then, almost angrily—"Yes, Signore."

But, to deprecate her anger, I kept her hand an instant, and then bent my venerable head and kissed it. I think I appeased her.

BOLOGNA, *14th.*—I left Florence on the 11th, and have been here these three days. Delightful old Italian town—but it lacks the charm of my Florentine secret.

I wrote that last entry five days ago, late at night, after coming back from Casa Salvi. I afterwards fell asleep in my chair; the night was half over when I woke up. Instead of going to bed, I stood a long time at the window, looking out at the river. It was a warm, still night, and the first faint streaks of sunrise were in the sky. Presently I heard a slow footstep beneath my window, and looking down, made out by the aid of a street-lamp that Stanmer was but just coming home. I called to him to come to my rooms, and, after an interval, he made his appearance.

"I want to bid you good-bye," I said; "I shall depart in the morning. Don't go to the trouble of saying you are sorry. Of course you are not; I must have bullied you immensely."

He made no attempt to say he was sorry, but he said he was very glad to have made my acquaintance.

"Your conversation," he said, with his little innocent air, "has been very suggestive."

"Have you found Camerino?" I asked, smiling.

"I have given up the search."

"Well," I said, "some day when you find that you have made a great mistake, remember I told you so."

He looked for a minute as if he were trying to anticipate that day by the exercise of his reason.

"Has it ever occurred to you that *you* may have made a great mistake?"

"Oh yes; everything occurs to one sooner or later."

That's what I said to him; but I didn't say that the question, pointed by his candid young countenance, had, for the moment, a greater force than it had ever had before.

And then he asked me whether, as things had turned out, I myself had been so especially happy.

PARIS, *December 17th*.—A note from young Stanmer, whom I saw in Florence—a remarkable little note, dated Rome, and worth transcribing.

"*My dear General,—I have it at heart to tell you that I was married a week ago to the Countess Salvi-Scarabelli. You talked me into a great muddle; but a month after that it was all very clear. Things that involve a risk are like the Christian faith; they must be seen from the inside.—Yours ever, E.S.*

"*P.S.—A fig for analogies unless you can find an analogy for my happiness!*"

His happiness makes him very clever. I hope it will last!—I mean his cleverness, not his happiness.

LONDON, *April 19th, 1877*.—Last night, at Lady H——'s, I met Edmund Stanmer, who married Bianca Salvi's daughter. I heard the other day that they had come to England. A handsome young fellow, with a fresh contented face. He reminded me of Florence, which I didn't pretend to forget; but it was rather awkward, for I remember I used to disparage that woman to him. I had a complete theory about her. But he didn't seem at all stiff; on the contrary, he appeared to enjoy our encounter. I asked him if his wife were there. I had to do that.

"Oh, yes, she's in one of the other rooms. Come and make her acquaintance; I want you to know her."

"You forget that I do know her."

"Oh, no, you don't; you never did." And he gave a little significant laugh.

I didn't feel like facing the *ci-devant* Scarabelli at that moment;

so I said that I was leaving the house, but that I would do myself the honour of calling upon his wife. We talked for a minute of something else, and then, suddenly, breaking off and looking at me, he laid his hand on my arm. I must do him the justice to say that he looks felicitous.

"Depend upon it, you were wrong!" he said.

"My dear young friend," I answered, "imagine the alacrity with which I concede it."

Something else again was spoken of, but in an instant he repeated his movement.

"Depend upon it you were wrong."

"I am sure the Countess has forgiven me," I said, "and in that case you ought to bear no grudge. As I have had the honour to say, I will call upon her immediately."

"I was not alluding to my wife," he answered. "I was thinking of your own story."

"My own story?"

"So many years ago. Was it not rather a mistake?"

I looked at him a moment; he's positively rosy.

"That's not a question to solve in a London crush."

And I turned away.

22nd.—I haven't yet called on the *ci-devant*; I am afraid of finding her at home. And that boy's words have been thrumming in my ears—"Depend upon it you were wrong. Wasn't it rather a mistake?" *Was* I wrong—*was* it a mistake? Was I too cautions—too suspicious—too logical? Was it really a protector she needed—a man who might have helped her? Would it have been for his benefit to believe in her and was her fault only that I had forsaken her? Was the poor woman very unhappy? God forgive me, how the questions come crowding in! If I marred her happiness, I certainly didn't make my own. And I might have made it—eh? That's a charming discovery for a man of my age!

Travelling Companions

I

THE MOST strictly impressive picture in Italy is incontestably the Last Supper of Leonardo at Milan. A part of its immense solemnity is doubtless due to its being one of the first of the great Italian masterworks that you encounter in coming down from the North. Another secondary source of interest resides in the very completeness of its decay. The mind finds a rare delight in filling each of its vacant spaces, effacing its rank defilement, and repairing, as far as possible, its sad disorder. Of the essential power and beauty of the work there can be no better evidence than this fact that, having lost so much, it has yet retained so much. An unquenchable elegance lingers in those vague outlines and incurable scars; enough remains to place you in sympathy with the unfathomable wisdom of the painter. The fresco covers a wall, the reader will remember, at the end of the former refectory of a monastery now suppressed, the precinct of which is occupied by a regiment of cavalry. Horses stamp, soldiers rattle their oaths, in the cloisters which once echoed to the sober tread of monastic sandals and the pious greetings of meek-voiced friars.

It was the middle of August, and summer sat brooding fiercely over the streets of Milan. The great brick-wrought dome of the church of St. Mary of the Graces rose black with the heat against the brazen sky. As my *fiacre* drew up in front of the church, I found another vehicle in possession of the little square of shade which carpeted the glaring pavement before the adjoining convent. I left the two drivers to share this advantage as they could, and made haste to enter the cooler presence of the Cenacolo. Here I found the occupants of the *fiacre* without, a young lady and an elderly man. Here also, besides the official who takes your tributary franc, sat a long-haired copyist, wooing back the silent secrets of the great fresco into the cheerfullest commonplaces of yellow and blue. The gentleman was earnestly watching this ingenious operation; the young lady sat with her eyes fixed on the picture, from which she failed to move them when I took my place on a line with her. I too, however, speedily became as unconscious of her presence as she of mine, and lost myself in the study of the work before us. A single glance had assured me that she was an American.

Since that day, I have seen all the great art treasures of Italy: I have seen Tintoretto at Venice, Michael Angelo at Florence and Rome, Correggio at Parma; but I have looked at no other picture with an emotion equal to that which rose within me as this great creation of Leonardo slowly began to dawn upon my intelligence from the tragical twilight of its ruin. A work so nobly conceived can never utterly die, so long as the half-dozen main lines of its design remain. Neglect and malice are less cunning than the genius of the great painter. It has stored away with masterly skill such a wealth of beauty as only perfect love and sympathy can fully detect. So, under my eyes, the restless ghost of the dead fresco returned to its mortal abode. From the beautiful central image of Christ I perceived its radiation right and left along the sadly broken line of the disciples. One by one, out of the depths of their grim dismemberment, the figures trembled into meaning and life, and the vast, serious beauty of the work stood revealed. What is the ruling force of this magnificent design? Is it art? is it science? is it sentiment? is it knowledge? I am sure I can't say; but in moments of doubt and depression I find it of excellent use to recall the great picture with all possible distinctness. Of all the works of man's hands it is the least superficial.

The young lady's companion finished his survey of the copyist's work and came and stood behind his chair. The reader will remember that a door has been rudely cut in the wall, a part of it entering the fresco.

"He hasn't got in that door," said the old gentleman, speaking apparently of the copyist.

The young lady was silent. "Well, my dear," he continued. "What do you think of it?"

The young girl gave a sigh. "I see it," she said.

"You see it, eh? Well, I suppose there is nothing more to be done."

The young lady rose slowly, drawing on her glove. As her eyes were still on the fresco, I was able to observe her. Beyond doubt she was American. Her age I fancied to be twenty-two. She was of middle stature, with a charming slender figure. Her hair was brown, her complexion fresh and clear. She wore a white piqué dress and a black lace shawl, and on her thick dark braids a hat with a purple feather. She was largely characterized by that physical delicacy and that personal elegance (each of them sometimes excessive) which seldom fail to betray my young countrywomen in Europe. The gentleman, who was obviously her father, bore the national stamp as plainly as she. A shrewd, firm, generous face, which told of many dealings with many men, of stocks and shares and current prices,—a face, moreover, in which there lingered the mellow afterglow of a sense of excellent claret. He was bald and grizzled, this perfect American, and he wore a short-bristled white moustache between the two hard wrinkles forming the sides of a triangle of which his mouth was the base and the ridge of his nose, where his eye-glass sat, the apex. In deference perhaps to this exotic growth, he was better dressed than is common with the typical American citizen, in a blue necktie, a white waistcoat, and a pair of gray trousers. As his daughter still lingered, he looked at me with an eye of sagacious conjecture.

"Ah, that beautiful, beautiful, beautiful Christ," said the young lady, in a tone which betrayed her words in spite of its softness. "O father, what a picture!"

"Hum!" said her father, "I don't see it."

"I must get a photograph," the young girl rejoined. She turned away and walked to the farther end of the hall, where the custodian presides at a table of photographs and prints. Meanwhile her father had perceived my Murray.

"English, sir?" he demanded.

"No, I'm an American, like yourself, I fancy."

"Glad to make your acquaintance, sir. From New York?"

"From New York. I have been absent from home, however, for a number of years."

"Residing in this part of the world?"

"No. I have been living in Germany. I have only just come into Italy."

"Ah, so have we. The young lady is my daughter. She is crazy about Italy. We were very nicely fixed at Interlaken, when suddenly she read in some confounded book or other that Italy should be seen in summer. So she dragged me over the mountains into this fiery furnace. I'm actually melting away. I have lost five pounds in three days."

I replied that the heat was indeed intense, but that I agreed with his daughter that Italy should be seen in summer. What could be pleasanter than the temperature of that vast cool hall?

"Ah, yes," said my friend; "I suppose we shall have plenty of this kind of thing. It makes no odds to me, so long as my poor girl has a good time."

"She seems," I remarked, "to be having a pretty good time with the photographs." In fact, she was comparing photographs with a great deal of apparent energy, while the salesman lauded his wares in the Italian manner. We strolled over to the table. The young girl was seemingly in treaty for a large photograph of the head of Christ, in which the blurred and fragmentary character of the original was largely intensified, though much of its exquisite pathetic beauty was also preserved. "They'll not think much of that at home," said the old gentleman.

"So much the worse for them," said his daughter, with an accent of delicate pity. With the photograph in her hand, she walked back to the fresco. Her father engaged in an English dialogue with the custodian. In the course of five minutes, wishing likewise to compare the copy and the original, I returned to the great picture. As I drew near it the young lady turned away. Her eyes then for the first time met my own. They were deep and dark and luminous,—I fancied streaming with tears. I watched her as she returned to the table. Her walk seemed to me peculiarly graceful; light, and rapid, and yet full of decision and dignity. A thrill of delight passed through my heart as I guessed at her moistened lids.

"Sweet fellow-countrywoman," I cried in silence, "you have the divine gift of feeling." And I returned to the fresco with a deepened sense of its virtue. When I turned around, my companions had left the room.

In spite of the great heat, I was prepared thoroughly to "do" Milan. In fact, I rather enjoyed the heat; it seemed to my Northern senses to deepen the Italian, the Southern, the local character of things. On that blazing afternoon, I have not forgotten, I went to the church of St. Ambrose, to the Ambrosian Library, to a dozen minor churches. Every step distilled a richer drop into the wholesome cup of pleasure. From my earliest manhood, beneath a German sky, I had dreamed of this Italian pilgrimage, and, after much waiting and working and planning, I had at last undertaken it in a spirit of fervent devotion. There had been moments in Germany when I fancied myself a clever man; but it now seemed to me that for the first time I really *felt* my intellect. Imagination, panting and exhausted, withdrew from the game; and Observation stepped into her place, trembling and glowing with open-eyed desire.

I had already been twice to the Cathedral, and had wandered through the clustering inner darkness of the high arcades which support those light-defying pinnacles and spires. Towards the close of the afternoon I found myself strolling once more over the great column-planted, altar-studded pavement, with the view of ascending to the roof. On presenting myself at the little door in the right transept, through which you gain admission to the upper regions, I perceived my late fellow-visitors of the fresco preparing apparently for an upward movement, but not without some reluctance on the paternal side. The poor gentleman had been accommodated with a chair, on which he sat fanning himself with his hat and looking painfully apoplectic. The sacristan meanwhile held open the door with an air of invitation. But my corpulent friend, with his thumb in his Murray, balked at the ascent. Recognizing me, his face expressed a sudden sense of vague relief.

"Have you been up, sir?" he inquired, groaningly.

I answered that I was about to ascend; and recalling then the fact, which I possessed rather as information than experience, that young American ladies may not improperly detach themselves on occasion from the parental side, I ventured to declare that, if my friend was unwilling to encounter the fatigue of mounting to the roof in person, I should be most happy, as a fellow-countryman, qualified already perhaps to claim a traveller's acquaintance, to accompany and assist his daughter.

"You're very good, sir," said the poor man; "I confess that I'm about played out. I'd far rather sit here and watch these pretty Italian ladies saying their prayers. Charlotte, what do you say?"

"Of course if you're tired I should be sorry to have you make the effort," said Charlotte. "But I believe the great thing is to see the view from the roof. I'm much obliged to the gentleman."

It was arranged accordingly that we should ascend together. "Good luck to you," cried my friend, "and mind you take good care of her."

Those who have rambled among the marble immensities of the summit of Milan Cathedral will hardly expect me to describe them. It is only when they have been seen as a complete concentric whole that they can be properly appreciated. It was not as a whole that I saw them; a week in Italy had assured me that I have not the architectural *coup d'œil*. In looking back on the scene into which we emerged from the stifling spiral of the ascent, I have chiefly a confused sense of an immense skyward elevation and a fierce blinding efflorescence of fantastic forms of marble. There, reared for the action of the sun, you find a vast marble world. The solid whiteness lies in mighty slabs along the iridescent slopes of nave and transept, like the lonely snow-fields of the higher Alps. It leaps and climbs and shoots and attacks the unsheltered blue with a keen and joyous incision. It meets the pitiless sun with a more than equal glow; the day falters, declines, expires, but the marble shines forever, unmelted and unintermittent. You will know what I mean if you have looked upward from the Piazza at midnight. With confounding frequency too, on some uttermost point of a pinnacle, its plastic force explodes into satisfied rest in some perfect flower of a figure. A myriad carven statues, known only to the circling air, are poised and niched beyond reach of human vision, the loss of which to mortal eyes is, I suppose, the gain of the Church and the Lord. Among all the jewelled shrines and overwrought tabernacles of Italy, I have seen no such magnificent waste of labor, no such glorious synthesis of cunning secrets. As you wander, sweating and blinking, over the changing levels of the edifice, your eye catches at a hundred points the little profile of a little saint, looking out into the dizzy air, a pair of folded hands praying to the bright immediate heavens, a sandalled monkish foot planted on the edge of the white abyss. And then, besides this mighty world of the great Cathedral itself, you possess the view of all green Lombardy,—vast, lazy Lombardy, resting from its Alpine upheavals.

My companion carried a little white umbrella, with a violet lining. Thus protected from the sun, she climbed and gazed with abundant courage and spirit. Her movements, her glance, her voice, were full of intelligent pleasure. Now that I could observe her closely, I saw that, though perhaps without regular beauty, she was yet, for youth, summer, and Italy, more than pretty enough. Owing to my residence in Germany, among Germans, in a small university town, Americans had come to have for me, in a large degree, the interest of novelty and remoteness. Of the charm of American women, in especial, I had formed a very high estimate, and I was more than ready to be led captive by the far-famed graces of their frankness and freedom. I already felt that in the young girl beside me there was a different quality of womanhood from any that I had recently known; a keenness, a maturity, a conscience, which deeply stirred my curiosity. It was positive, not negative maidenhood.

"You're an American," I said, as we stepped to look at the distance.

"Yes; and you?" In her voice alone the charm faltered. It was high, thin, and nervous.

"Oh, happily, I'm also one."

"I shouldn't have thought so. I should have taken you for a German."

"By education I am a German. I knew you were an American the moment I looked at you."

"I suppose so. It seems that American women are easily recognized. But don't talk about America." She paused and swept her dark eye over the whole immensity of prospect. "This is Italy," she cried, "Italy, Italy!"

"Italy indeed. What do you think of the Leonardo?"

"I fancy there can be only one feeling about it. It must be the saddest and finest of all pictures. But I know nothing of art. I have seen nothing yet but that lovely Raphael in the Brera."

"You have a vast deal before you. You're going southward, I suppose."

"Yes, we are going directly to Venice. There I shall see Titian."

"Titian and Paul Veronese."

"Yes, I can hardly believe it. Have you ever been in a gondola?"

"No; this is my first visit to Italy."

"Ah, this is all new, then, to you as well."

"Divinely new," said I, with fervor.

She glanced at me, with a smile,—a ray of friendly pleasure in my pleasure. "And you are not disappointed!"

"Not a jot. I'm too good a German."

"I'm too good an American. I live at Araminta, New Jersey!"

We thoroughly "did" the high places of the church, concluding with an ascent into the little gallery of the central spire. The view from this spot is beyond all words, especially the view toward the long mountain line which shuts out the North. The sun was sinking: clear and serene upon their blue foundations, the snow-peaks sat clustered and scattered, and shrouded in silence and light. To the south the long shadows fused and multiplied, and the bosky Lombard flats melted away into perfect Italy. This prospect offers a great emotion to the Northern traveller. A vague, delicious impulse of conquest stirs in his heart. From his dizzy vantage-point, as he looks down at her, beautiful, historic, exposed, he embraces the whole land in the far-reaching range of his desire. "That is Monte Rosa," I said; "that is the Simplon pass; there is the triple glitter of those lovely lakes."

"Poor Monte Rosa," said my companion.

"I'm sure I never thought of Monte Rosa as an object of pity."

"You don't know what she represents. She represents the genius of the North. There she stands, frozen and fixed, resting her head upon that mountain wall, looking over at this lovely southern world and yearning towards it forever in vain."

"It is very well she can't come over. She would melt."

"Very true. She is beautiful, too, in her own way. I mean to fancy that I am her chosen envoy, and that I have come up here to receive her blessing."

I made an attempt to point out a few localities. "Yonder lies Venice, out of sight. In the interval are a dozen divine little towns. I hope to visit them all. I shall ramble all day in their streets and churches, their little museums, and their great palaces. In the evening I shall sit at the door of a café in the little piazza, scanning some lovely civic edifice in the moonlight, and saying, 'Ah! this is Italy!'"

"You gentlemen are certainly very happy. I'm afraid we must go straight to Venice."

"Your father insists upon it?"

"He wishes it. Poor father! in early life he formed the habit of being in a hurry, and he can't break it even now, when, being out of business, he has nothing on earth to do."

"But in America I thought daughters insisted as well as fathers."

The young girl looked at me, half serious, half smiling. "Have you a mother?" she asked; and then, blushing the least bit at her directness and without waiting for an answer, "This is not America," she said. "I should like to think I might become for a while a creature of Italy."

Somehow I felt a certain contagion in her momentary flash of frankness. "I strongly suspect," I said, "that you are American to the depths of your soul, and that you'll never be anything else; I hope not."

In this hope of mine there was perhaps a little impertinence; but my companion looked at me with a gentle smile, which seemed to hint that she forgave it. "You, on the other hand," she said, "are a perfect German, I fancy; and you'll never be anything else."

"I am sure I wish with all my heart," I answered, "to be a good American. I'm open to conversion. Try me."

"Thank you; I haven't the ardour; I'll make you over to my

father. We mustn't forget, by the way, that he is waiting for us."

We did forget it, however, awhile longer. We came down from the tower and made our way to the balustrade which edges the front of the edifice, and looked down on the city and the piazza below. Milan had, to my sense, a peculiar charm of temperate gayety,—the softness of the South without its laxity; and I felt as if I could gladly spend a month there. The common life of the streets was beginning to stir and murmur again, with the subsiding heat and the approaching night. There came up into our faces a delicious emanation as from the sweetness of Transalpine life. At the little balconies of the windows, beneath the sloping awnings, with their feet among the crowded flower-pots and their plump bare arms on the iron rails, lazy, dowdy Italian beauties would appear, still drowsy with the broken *siesta*. Beautiful, slim young officers had begun to dot the pavement, glorious with their clanking swords, their brown moustaches, and their legs of azure. In gentle harmony with these, various ladies of Milan were issuing forth to enjoy the cool; elegant, romantic, provoking, in short black dresses and lace mantillas depending from their *chignons*, with a little cloud of powder artfully enhancing the darkness of their hair and eyes. How it all wasn't Germany! how it couldn't have been Araminta, New Jersey! "It's the South, the South," I kept repeating,—"the South in nature, in man, in manners." It was a brighter world. "It's the South," I said to my companion. "Don't you feel it in all your nerves?"

"O, it's very pleasant," she said.

"We must forget all our cares and duties and sorrows. We must go in for the beautiful. Think of this great trap for the sunbeams, in this city of yellows and russets and crimsons, of liquid vowels and glancing smiles being, like one of our Northern cathedrals, a temple to Morality and Conscience. It doesn't belong to heaven, but to earth,—to love and light and pleasure."

My friend was silent a moment. "I'm glad I'm not a Catholic," she said at last. "Come, we must go down."

We found the interior of the Cathedral delightfully cool and shadowy. The young lady's father was not at our place of ingress, and we began to walk through the church in search of him. We met a number of Milanese ladies, who charmed us with their sombre elegance and the Spanish romance of their veils. With these pale penitents and postulants my companion had a lingering sisterly sympathy.

"Don't you wish you were a Catholic now?" I asked. "It would be so pleasant to wear one of those lovely mantillas."

"The mantillas are certainly becoming," she said. "But who knows what horrible old-world sorrows and fears and remorses they cover? Look at this person." We were standing near the great altar. As she spoke, a woman rose from her knees, and as she drew the folds of her lace mantle across her bosom, fixed her large dark eyes on us with a peculiar significant intensity. She was of less than middle age, with a pale, haggard face, a certain tarnished elegance of dress, and a remarkable nobleness of gesture and carriage. She came towards us, with an odd mixture, in her whole expression, of decency and defiance. "Are you English?" she said in Italian. "You are very pretty. Is he a brother or a lover?"

"He is neither," said I, affecting a tone of rebuke.

"Neither? only a friend! You are very happy to have a friend, Signorina. Ah, you are pretty! You were watching me at my prayers just now; you thought me very curious, apparently. I don't care. You may see me here any day. But I devoutly hope you may never have to pray such bitter, bitter prayers as mine. A thousand excuses." And she went her way.

"What in the world does she mean?" said my companion.

"Monte Rosa," said I, "was the genius of the North. This poor woman is the genius of the Picturesque. She shows us the essential misery that lies behind it. It's not an unwholesome lesson to receive at the outset. Look at her sweeping down the aisle. What a poise of the head! The picturesque is handsome, all the same."

"I do wonder what is her trouble," murmured the young girl. "She has swept away an illusion in the folds of those black garments."

"Well," said I, "here is a solid fact to replace it." My eyes had just lighted upon the object of our search. He sat in a chair, half tilted back against a pillar. His chin rested on his shirt-bosom, and his hands were folded together over his waistcoat, where it most protruded. Shirt and waistcoat rose and fell with visible, audible regularity. I wandered apart and left his daughter to deal with him. When she had fairly aroused him, he thanked me heartily for my care of the young lady, and expressed the wish that we might meet again. "We start to-morrow for Venice," he said. "I want awfully to get a whiff of the sea-breeze and to see if there is anything to be got out of a gondola."

As I expected also to be in Venice before many days, I had little doubt of our meeting. In consideration of this circumstance, my friend proposed that we should exchange cards; which we accordingly did, then and there, before the high altar, above the gorgeous chapel which enshrines the relics of St. Charles Borromeus. It was thus that I learned his name to be Mr. Mark Evans.

"Take a few notes for us!" said Miss Evans, as I shook her hand in farewell.

I spent the evening, after dinner, strolling among the crowded streets of the city, tasting of Milanese humanity. At the door of a café I perceived Mr. Evans seated at a little round table. He seemed to have discovered the merits of absinthe. I wondered where he had left his daughter. She was in her room, I fancied, writing her journal.

The fortnight which followed my departure from Milan was in all respects memorable and delightful. With an interest that hourly deepened as I read, I turned the early pages of the enchanting romance of Italy. I carried out in detail the programme which I had sketched for Miss Evans. Those few brief days, as I look back on them, seem to me the sweetest, fullest, calmest of my life. All personal passions, all restless egotism, all worldly hopes, regrets, and fears were stilled and absorbed in the steady perception of the material present. It exhaled the pure essence of romance. What words can reproduce the picture which these Northern Italian towns project upon a sympathetic retina? They are shabby, deserted, dreary, decayed, unclean. In those August days the southern sun poured into them with a fierceness which might have seemed fatal to any lurking shadow of picturesque mystery. But taking them as cruel time had made them and left them, I found in them an immeasurable instruction and charm. My perception seemed for the first time to live a sturdy creative life of its own. How it fed upon the mouldy crumbs of the festal past! I have always thought the observant faculty a windy impostor, so long as it refuses to pocket pride and doff its bravery and crawl on all-fours, if need be, into the unillumined corners and crannies of life. In these dead cities of Verona, Mantua, Padua, how life had revelled and postured in its strength! How sentiment and passion had blossomed and flowered! How much of history had been performed! What a wealth of mortality had ripened and decayed! I have never elsewhere got so deep an impression of the social secrets of mankind. In England, even, in those verdure-stifled haunts of domestic peace which muffle the sounding chords of British civilization, one has a fainter sense of the possible movement and fruition of individual character. Beyond a certain point you fancy it merged in the general medium of duty, business, and politics. In Italy, in spite of your knowledge of the strenuous public conscience which once inflamed these compact little states, the unapplied, spontaneous moral life of society seems to have been more active and more subtle. I walked about with a volume of Stendhal in my pocket; at every step I gathered some lingering testimony to the exquisite vanity of ambition.

But the great emotion, after all, was to feel myself among scenes in which art had ranged so freely. It had often enough been bad, but it had never ceased to be art. An invincible instinct of beauty had presided at life,—an instinct often ludicrously crude and primitive. Wherever I turned I found a vital principle of grace,—from the smile of a chambermaid to the curve of an arch. My memory reverts with an especial tenderness to certain hours in the dusky, faded saloons of those vacant, ruinous palaces which boast of "collections." The pictures are frequently poor, but the visitor's impression is generally rich. The brick-tiled floors are bare; the doors lack paint; the great windows, curtains; the chairs and tables have lost their gilding and their damask drapery; but the ghost of a graceful aristocracy treads at your side and does the melancholy honours of the abode with a dignity that brooks no sarcasm. You feel that art and piety here have been blind, generous instincts. You are reminded in persuasive accents of the old personal regimen in human affairs. Certain pictures are veiled and curtained *virginibus puerisque*. Through these tarnished halls lean and patient abbés led their youthful virginal pupils. Have you read Stendhal's *Chartreuse de Parme*? There was such a gallery in the palace of the Duchess of San Severino. After a long day of strolling, lounging, and staring, I found a singularly perfect pleasure in sitting at the door of a café in the warm star-light, eating an ice and making an occasional experiment in the way of talk with my neighbours. I recall with peculiar fondness and delight three sweet sessions in the delicious Piazza dei Signori at Verona. The Piazza is small, compact, private almost, accessible only to pedestrians, paved with great slabs which have known none but a gentle human tread. On one side of it rises in elaborate elegance and grace, above its light arched *loggia*, the image-bordered mass of the ancient palace of the Council; facing this stand two sterner, heavier buildings, dedicated to municipal offices and to the lodgement of soldiers. Step through the archway which leads out of the Piazza and you will find a vast quadrangle with a staircase climbing sunward, along the wall, a row of gendarmes sitting in the shade, a group of soldiers cleaning their muskets, a dozen persons of either sex leaning downward from the open windows. At one end of the little square rose into the pale darkness the high slender shaft of a brick campanile; in the centre glittered steadily a colossal white statue of Dante. Behind this statue was the Caffè Dante, where on three successive days I sat till midnight, feeling the scene, learning its sovereign "distinction." But of Verona I shall not pretend to speak. As I drew near Venice I began to feel a soft impatience, an expectant tremor of the heart. The day before reaching it I spent at Vicenza. I wandered all day through the streets, of course, looking at Palladio's palaces and enjoying them in defiance of reason and Ruskin. They seemed to me essentially rich and palatial. In the evening I resorted, as usual, to the city's generous heart, the decayed ex-glorious Piazza. This spot at Vicenza affords you a really soul-stirring premonition of Venice. There is no Byzantine Basilica and no Ducal Palace; but there is an immense impressive hall of council, and a soaring campanile, and there are two discrowned columns telling of defeated Venetian dominion. Here

I seated myself before a café door, in a group of gossiping votaries of the Southern night. The tables being mostly occupied, I had some difficulty in finding one. In a short time I perceived a young man walking through the crowd, seeking where he might bestow himself. Passing near me, he stopped and asked me with irresistible grace if he might share my table. I cordially assented; he sat down and ordered a glass of sugar and water. He was of about my own age, apparently, and full of the opulent beauty of the greater number of young Italians. His dress was simple even to shabbiness: he might have been a young prince in disguise, a Haroun-al-Raschid. With small delay we engaged in conversation. My companion was boyish, modest, and gracious; he nevertheless discoursed freely on the things of Vicenza. He was so good as to regret that we had not met earlier in the day; it would have given him such pleasure to accompany me on my tour of the city. He was passionately fond of art: he was in fact an artist. Was I fond of pictures? Was I inclined to purchase? I answered that I had no desire to purchase modern pictures, that in fact I had small means to purchase any. He informed me that he had a beautiful ancient work which, to his great regret, he found himself compelled to sell; a most divine little Correggio. Would I do him the favour to look at it? I had small belief in the value of this unrenowned masterpiece; but I felt a kindness for the young painter. I consented to have him call for me the next morning and take me to his house, where for two hundred years, he assured me, the work had been jealously preserved.

He came punctually, beautiful, smiling, shabby, as before. After a ten minutes' walk we stopped before a gaudy half-palazzo which rejoiced in a vague Palladian air. In the basement, looking on the court, lived my friend; with his mother, he informed me, and his sister. He ushered me in, through a dark antechamber, into which, through a gaping kitchen door, there gushed a sudden aroma of onions. I found myself in a high, half-darkened saloon. One of the windows was open into the court, from which the light entered verdantly through a row of flowering plants. In an arm-chair near the window sat a young girl in a dressing-gown, empty-handed, pale, with wonderful eyes, apparently an invalid. At her side stood a large elderly woman in a rusty black silk gown, with an agreeable face, flushed a little, apparently with the expectation of seeing me. The young man introduced them as his mother and his sister. On a table near the window, propped upright in such a way as to catch the light, was a small picture in a heavy frame. I proceeded to examine it. It represented in simple composition a Madonna and Child; the mother facing you, pressing the infant to her bosom, faintly smiling, and looking out of the picture with a solemn sweetness. It was pretty, it was good; but it was not Correggio. There was indeed a certain suggestion of his exquisite touch; but it was a likeness merely, and not the precious reality. One fact, however, struck swiftly home to my consciousness: the face of the Madonna bore a singular resemblance to that of Miss Evans. The lines, the character, the expression, were the same; the faint half-thoughtful smile was hers, the feminine frankness and gentle confidence of the brow, from which the dark hair waved back with the same even abundance. All this, in the Madonna's face, was meant for heaven; and on Miss Evans's in a fair degree, probably, for earth. But the mutual likeness was, nevertheless, perfect, and it quickened my interest in the picture to a point which the intrinsic merit of the work would doubtless have failed to justify; although I confess that I was now not slow to discover a great deal of agreeable painting in it.

"But I doubt of its being a Correggio," said I.

"A Correggio, I give you my word of honour, sir!" cried my young man.

"*Ecco!* my son's word of honour," cried his mother.

"I don't deny," I said, "that it is a very pretty work. It is perhaps Parmigianino."

"O no, sir," the elder insisted, "a true Correggio! We have had it two hundred years! Try another light; you will see. A true Correggio! Isn't it so, my daughter?"

The young man put his arm in mine, played his fingers airily over the picture, and whispered of a dozen beauties.

"O, I grant you," said I, "it's a very pretty picture." As I looked at it I felt the dark eyes of the young girl in the arm-chair fixed upon me with almost unpleasant intensity. I met her gaze for a moment:

I found in it a strange union of defiant pride and sad despondent urgency.

"What do you ask for the picture?" I said.

There was a silence.

"Speak, *madre mia*," said the young man.

"*La senta!*" and the lady played with her broken fan. "We should like you to name a price."

"O, if I named a price, it would not be as for a Correggio. I can't afford to buy Correggios. If this were a real Correggio, you would be rich. You should go to a duke, a prince, not to me."

"We would be rich! Do you hear, my children? We are very poor, sir. You have only to look at us. Look at my poor daughter. She was once beautiful, fresh, gay. A year ago she fell ill: a long story, sir, and a sad one. We have had doctors; they have ordered five thousand things. My daughter gets no better. There it is, sir. We are very poor."

The young girl's look confirmed her mother's story. That she had been beautiful I could easily believe; that she was ill was equally apparent. She was still remarkable indeed for a touching, hungry, unsatisfied grace. She remained silent and motionless, with her eyes fastened upon my face. I again examined the pretended Correggio. It was wonderfully like Miss Evans. The young American rose up in my mind with irresistible vividness and grace. How she seemed to glow with strength, freedom, and joy, beside this sombre, fading, Southern sister! It was a happy thought that, under the benediction of her image, I might cause a ray of healing sunshine to fall at this poor girl's feet.

"Have you ever tried to sell the picture before?"

"Never!" said the old lady, proudly. "My husband had it from his father. If we have made up our minds to part with it now,— most blessed little Madonna!—it is because we have had an intimation from heaven."

"From heaven?"

"From heaven, Signore. My daughter had a dream. She dreamed that a young stranger came to Vicenza, and that he wandered about the streets saying, 'Where, ah where, is my blessed Lady?' Some told him in one church, and some told him in another. He went into all the churches and lifted all the curtains, giving great fees to the sacristans! But he always came out shaking his head and repeating his question, 'Where is my blessed Lady? I have come from over the sea, I have come to Italy to find her!' " The woman delivered herself of this recital with a noble florid unction and a vast redundancy, to my Northern ear, of delightful liquid sounds. As she paused momentarily, her daughter spoke for the first time.

"And then I fancied," said the young girl, "that I heard his voice pausing under my window at night. 'His blessed Lady is here,' I said, 'we must not let him lose her.' So I called my brother and bade him go forth in search of you. I dreamed that he brought you back. We made an altar with candles and lace and flowers, and on it we placed the little picture. The stranger had light hair, light eyes, a flowing beard like you. He kneeled down before the little Madonna and worshipped her. We left him at his devotions and went away. When we came back the candles on the altar were out : the Madonna was gone, too; but in its place there burned a bright pure light. It was a purse of gold!"

"What a very pretty story!" said I. "How many pieces were there in the purse?"

The young man burst into a laugh. "Twenty thousand!" he said.

I made my offer for the picture. It was esteemed generous apparently; I was cordially thanked. As it was inconvenient, however, to take possession of the work at that moment, I agreed to pay down but half the sum, reserving the other half to the time of delivery. When I prepared to take my departure the young girl rose from her chair and enabled me to measure at once her weakness and her beauty. "Will you come back for the picture yourself?" she asked.

"Possibly. I should like to see you again. You must get better."

"O, I shall never get better."

"I can't believe that. I shall perhaps have a dream to tell you!"

"I shall soon be in heaven. I shall send you one."

"Listen to her!" cried the mother. "But she is already an angel."

With a farewell glance at my pictured Madonna I departed. My visit to this little Vicenza household had filled me with a painful, indefinable sadness. So beautiful they all were, so civil, so charming, and yet so mendacious and miserable! As I hurried along in the train toward the briny cincture of Venice, my heart was heavy with the image of that sombre, dying Italian maiden. Her face haunted me. What fatal wrong had she suffered? What hidden sorrow had blasted the freshness of her youth? As I began to smell the nearing Adriatic, my fancy bounded forward to claim asylum in the calmer presence of my bright American friend. I have no space to tell the story of my arrival in Venice and my first impressions. Mr. Evans had not mentioned his hotel. He was not at the Hotel de l'Europe, whither I myself repaired. If he was still in Venice, however, I foresaw that we should not fail to meet. The day succeeding my arrival I spent in a restless fever of curiosity and delight, now lost in the sensuous ease of my gondola, now lingering in charmed devotion before a canvas of Tintoretto or Paul Veronese. I exhausted three gondoliers and saw all Venice in a passionate fury and haste. I wished to probe its fulness and learn at once the best—or the worst. Late in the afternoon I disembarked at the Piazzetta and took my way haltingly and gazingly to the many-domed Basilica,—that shell of silver with a lining of marble. It was that enchanting Venetian hour when the ocean-touching sun sits melting to death, and the whole still air seems to glow with the soft effusion of his golden substance. Within the church, the deep brown shadow-masses, the heavy thick-tinted air, the gorgeous composite darkness, reigned in richer, quainter, more fantastic gloom than my feeble pen can reproduce the likeness of. From those rude concavities of dome and semi-dome, where the multitudinous facets of pictorial mosaic shimmer and twinkle in their own dull brightness; from the vast antiquity of innumerable marbles, incrusting the walls in roughly mated slabs, cracked and polished and triple-tinted with eternal service; from the wavy carpet of compacted stone, where a thousand once-bright fragments glimmer through the long attrition of idle feet and devoted knees; from sombre gold and mellow alabaster, from porphyry and malachite, from long dead crystal and the sparkle of undying lamps,—there proceeds a dense rich atmosphere of splendour and sanctity which transports the half-stupefied traveller to the age of a simpler and more awful faith. I wandered for half an hour beneath those reverted cups of scintillating darkness, stumbling on the great stony swells of the pavement as I gazed upward at the long mosaic saints who curve gigantically with the curves of dome and ceiling. I had left Europe; I was in the East. An overwhelming sense of the sadness of man's spiritual history took possession of my heart. The clustering picturesque shadows about me seemed to represent the darkness of a past from which he had slowly and painfully struggled. The great mosaic images, hideous, grotesque, inhuman, glimmered like the cruel spectres of early superstitions and terrors. There came over me, too, a poignant conviction of the ludicrous folly of the idle spirit of travel. How with Murray and an opera-glass it strolls and stares where omniscient angels stand diffident and sad! How blunted and stupid are its senses! How trivial and superficial its imaginings! To this builded sepulchre of trembling hope and dread, this monument of mighty passions, I had wandered in search of pictorial effects. O vulgarity! Of course I remained, nevertheless, still curious of effects. Suddenly I perceived a very agreeable one. Kneeling on a low *prie-dieu*, with her hands clasped, a lady was gazing upward at the great mosaic Christ in the dome of the choir. She wore a black lace shawl and a purple hat. She was Miss Evans. Her attitude slightly puzzled me. Was she really at her devotions, or was she only playing at prayer? I walked to a distance, so that she might have time to move before I addressed her. Five minutes afterwards, however, she was in the same position. I walked slowly towards her, and as I approached her attracted her attention. She immediately recognized me and smiled and bowed, without moving from her place.

"I saw you five minutes ago," I said, "but I was afraid of interrupting your prayers."

"O, they were only half-prayers," she said.

"Half-prayers are pretty well for one who only the other day was thanking Heaven that she was not a Catholic."

"Half-prayers are no prayers. I'm not a Catholic yet."

Her father, she told me, had brought her to the church, but had returned on foot to the hotel for his pocket-book. They were to dine at one of the restaurants in the Piazza. Mr. Evans was vastly contented with Venice, and spent his days and nights in gondolas. Awaiting his return, we wandered over the church. Yes, incontestably, Miss Evans resembled my little Vicenza picture. She looked a little pale with the heat and the constant nervous tension of sightseeing; but she pleased me now as effectually as she had pleased me before. There was an even deeper sweetness in the freedom and breadth of her utterance and carriage. I felt more even than before that she was an example of woman active, not of woman passive. We strolled through the great Basilica in serious, charmed silence. Miss Evans told me that she had been there much: she seemed to know it well. We went into the dark Baptistery and sat down on a bench against the wall, trying to discriminate in the vaulted dimness the harsh medieval reliefs behind the altar and the mosaic Crucifixion above it.

"Well," said I, "what has Venice done for you?"

"Many things. Tired me a little, saddened me, charmed me."

"How have you spent your time?"

"As people spend it. After breakfast we get into our gondola and remain in it pretty well till bedtime. I believe I know every canal, every canaletto, in Venice. You must have learned already how sweet it is to lean back under the awning, to feel beneath you that steady, liquid lapse, to look out at all this bright, sad elegance of ruin. I have been reading two or three of George Sand's novels. Do you know *La Dernière Aldini*? I fancy a romance in every palace."

"The reality of Venice seems to me to exceed all romance. It's romance enough simply to be here."

"Yes; but how brief and transient a romance!"

" Well," said I, "we shall certainly cease to be here, but we shall never cease to have been here. You are not to leave directly, I hope."

"In the course of ten days or a fortnight, we go to Florence."

"And then to Rome?"

"To Rome and Naples, and then by sea, probably, to Genoa, and thence to Nice and Paris. We must be at home by the new year. And you?"

"I hope to spend the winter in Italy."

"Are you never coming home again?"

"By no means. I shall probably return in the spring. But I wish you, too, were going to remain."

"You are very good. My father pronounces it impossible. I have only to make the most of it while I'm here."

"Are you going back to Araminta?"

Miss Evans was silent a moment. "O, don't ask!" she said.

"What kind of a place is Araminta?" I asked, maliciously.

Again she was silent. "That is John the Baptist on the cover of the basin," she said, at last, rising to her feet, with a light laugh.

On emerging from the Baptistery we found Mr. Evans, who greeted me cordially and insisted on my coming to dine with them. I think most fondly of our little dinner. We went to the Caffè Quadri and occupied a table beside an open window, looking out into the Piazza, which was beginning to fill with evening loungers and listeners to the great band of music in the centre. Miss Evans took off her hat and sat facing me in friendly silence. Her father sustained the larger burden of conversation. He seemed to feel its weight, however, as the dinner proceeded and when he had attacked his second bottle of wine. Miss Evans then questioned me about my journey from Milan. I told her the whole story, and felt that I infused into it a great deal of colour and heat. She sat charming me forward with her steady, listening smile. For the first time in my life I felt the magic of sympathy. After dinner we went down into the Piazza and established ourselves at one of Florian's tables. Night had become perfect; the music was magnificent. At a neighbouring table was a group of young Venetian gentlemen, splendid in dress, after the manner of their kind, and glorious with the wondrous physical glory of the Italian race.

"They only need velvet and satin and plumes," I said, "to be subjects for Titian and Paul Veronese."

They sat rolling their dark eyes and kissing their white hands at passing friends, with smiles that were like the moon-flashes on the Adriatic.

"They are beautiful exceedingly," said Miss Evans; "the most beautiful creatures in the world, except—"

"Except, you mean, this other gentleman."

She assented. The person of whom I had spoken was a young

man who was just preparing to seat himself at a vacant table. A lady and gentleman, elderly persons, had passed near him and recognized him, and he had uncovered himself and now stood smiling and talking. They were all genuine Anglo-Saxons. The young man was rather short of stature, but firm and compact. His hair was light and crisp, his eye a clear blue, his face and neck violently tanned by exposure to the sun. He wore a pair of small blond whiskers.

"Do you call him beautiful?" demanded Mr. Evans. " He reminds me of myself when I was his age. Indeed, he looks like you, sir."

"He's not beautiful," said Miss Evans, "but he is handsome."

The young man's face was full of decision and spirit; his whole figure had been moulded by action, tempered by effort. He looked simple and keen, upright, downright.

"Is he English?" asked Miss Evans, "or American?"

"He is both," I said, "or either. He is made of that precious clay that is common to the whole English-speaking race."

"He's American."

"Very possibly," said I; and indeed we never learned. I repeat the incident because I think it has a certain value in my recital. Before we separated I expressed the hope that we might meet again on the morrow.

"It's very kind of you to propose it," said Miss Evans; "but you'll thank us for refusing. Take my advice, as for an old Venetian, and spend the coming three days alone. How can you enjoy Tintoretto and Bellini, when you are racking your brains for small talk for me?"

"With you, Miss Evans, I shouldn't talk small. But you shape my programme with a liberal hand. At the end of three days, pray, where will you be?"

They would still be in Venice, Mr. Evans declared. It was a capital hotel, and then those jolly gondolas! I was unable to impeach the wisdom of the young girl's proposition. To be so wise, it seemed to me, was to be extremely charming.

For three days, accordingly, I wandered about alone. I often thought of Miss Evans and I often fancied I should enjoy certain

great pictures none the less for that deep associated contemplation
and those fine emanations of assent and dissent which I should
have known in her society. I wandered far; I penetrated deep, it
seemed to me, into the heart of Venetian power. I shook myself free
of the sad and sordid present, and embarked on that silent
contemplative sea whose irresistible tides expire at the base of the
mighty canvases in the Scuola di San Rocco. But on my return to
the hither shore, I always found my sweet young countrywoman
waiting to receive me. If Miss Evans had been an immense
coquette, she could not have proceeded more cunningly than by
this injunction of a three days' absence. During this period, in my
imagination, she increased tenfold in value. I don't mean to say
that there were not hours together when I quite forgot her, and
when I had no heart but for Venice and the lessons of Venice, for
the sea and sky and the great painters and builders. But when my
mind had executed one of these great passages of appreciation, it
turned with a sudden sense of solitude and lassitude to those
gentle hopes, those fragrant hints of intimacy, which clustered
about the person of my friend. She remained modestly uneclipsed
by the women of Titian. She was as deeply a woman as they, and yet
so much more of a person; as fit as the broadest and blondest to be
loved for herself, yet full of serene superiority as an active friend.
To the old, old sentiment what an exquisite modern turn she might
give! I so far overruled her advice as that, with her father, we made
a trio every evening, after the day's labours, at one of Florian's
tables. Mr. Evans drank absinthe and discoursed upon the glories
of our common country, of which he declared it was high time I
should make the acquaintance. He was not the least of a bore:
I relished him vastly. He was in many ways an excellent repres-
entative American. Without taste, without culture or polish, he
nevertheless produced an impression of substance in character,
keenness in perception, and intensity in will, which effectually
redeemed him from vulgarity. It often seemed to me, in fact, that
his good-humoured tolerance and easy morality, his rank self-
confidence, his nervous decision and vivacity, his fearlessness of
either gods or men, combined in proportions of which the union
might have been very fairly termed aristocratic. His voice, I admit,

was of the nose, nasal; but possibly, in the matter of utterance, one eccentricity is as good as another. At all events, with his clear, cold gray eye, with that just faintly impudent, more than level poise of his ample chin, with those two hard lines which flanked the bristling wings of his gray moustache, with his general expression of unchallenged security and practical aptitude and incurious scorn of tradition, he impressed the sensitive beholder as a man of incontestable force. He was entertaining, too, partly by wit and partly by position. He was weak only in his love of absinthe. After his first glass he left his chair and strolled about the piazza, looking for possible friends and superbly unconscious of possible enemies. His daughter sat back in her chair, her arms folded, her ungloved hands sustaining them, her prettiness half defined, her voice enhanced and subdued by the gas-tempered starlight. We had infinite talk. Without question, she had an admirable feminine taste: she was worthy to know Venice. I remember telling her so in a sudden explosion of homage. "You are really worthy to know Venice, Miss Evans. We must learn to know it together. Who knows what hidden treasures we may help each other to find?"

II

AT the end of my three days' probation, I spent a week constantly with my friends. Our mornings were, of course, devoted to churches and galleries, and in the late afternoon we passed and repassed along the Grand Canal or betook ourselves to the Lido. By this time Miss Evans and I had become thoroughly intimate; we had learned to know Venice together, and the knowledge had helped us to know each other. In my own mind, Charlotte Evans and Venice had played the game most effectively into each other's hands. If my fancy had been called upon to paint her portrait, my fancy would have sketched her with a background of sunset-flushed palace wall, with a faint reflected light from the green lagoon playing up into her face. And if I had wished to sketch a

Venetian scene, I should have painted it from an open window, with a woman leaning against the casement,—as I had often seen her lean from a window in her hotel. At the end of a week we went one afternoon to the Lido, timing our departure so as to allow us to return at sunset. We went over in silence, Mr. Evans sitting with reverted head, blowing his cigar-smoke against the dazzling sky, which told so fiercely of sea and summer; his daughter motionless and thickly veiled; I facing them, feeling the broken swerve of our gondola, and watching Venice grow level and rosy beyond the liquid interval. Near the landing-place on the hither side of the Lido is a small *trattoria* for the refreshment of visitors. An arbour outside the door, a horizontal vine checkering still further a dirty table-cloth, a pungent odour of *frittata*, an admiring circle of gondoliers and beggars, are the chief attractions of this suburban house of entertainment,—attractions sufficient, however, to have arrested the inquisitive steps of an elderly American gentleman, in whom Mr. Evans speedily recognized a friend of early years, a comrade in affairs. A hearty greeting ensued. This worthy man had ordered dinner: he besought Mr. Evans at least to sit down and partake of a bottle of wine. My friend vacillated between his duties as a father and the prospect of a rich old-boyish revival of the delectable interests of home; but his daughter graciously came to his assistance. "Sit down with Mr. Munson, talk till you are tired, and then walk over to the beach and find us. We shall not wander beyond call."

She and I accordingly started slowly for a stroll along the barren strand which averts its shining side from Venice and takes the tides of the Adriatic. The Lido has for me a peculiar melancholy charm, and I have often wondered that I should have felt the presence of beauty in a spot so destitute of any exceptional elements of beauty. For beyond the fact that it knows the changing moods and hues of the Adriatic, this narrow strip of sand-stifled verdure has no very rare distinction. In my own country I know many a sandy beach, and many a stunted copse, and many a tremulous ocean line of little less purity and breadth of composition, with far less magical interest. The secret of the Lido is simply your sense of adjacent Venice. It is the salt-sown garden of the city of the sea. Hither came short-paced Venetians for a meagre taste of *terra firma*, or for a wider glimpse of their parent ocean. Along a narrow line in the middle of the island are market-gardens and breeze-twisted orchards, and a hint of hedges and lanes and inland greenery. At one end is a series of low fortifications duly embanked and moated and sentinelled. Still beyond these, half over-drifted with sand and over-clambered with rank grasses and coarse thick shrubbery, are certain quaintly lettered funereal slabs, tombs of former Jews of Venice. Toward these we slowly wandered and sat down in the grass. Between the sand-heaps, which shut out the beach, we saw in a dozen places the blue agitation of the sea. Over all the scene there brooded the deep bright sadness of early autumn. I lay at my companion's feet and wondered whether I was in love. It seemed to me that I had never been so happy in my life. They say, I know, that to be in love is not pure happiness; that in the mood of the unconfessed, unaccepted lover there is an element of poignant doubt and pain. Should I at once confess myself and taste of the perfection of bliss? It seemed to me that I cared very little for the meaning of her reply. I only wanted to talk of love; I wanted in some manner to enjoy in that atmosphere of romance the woman who was so blessedly fair and wise. It seemed to me that all the agitation of fancy, the excited sense of beauty, the fervour and joy and sadness begotten by my Italian wanderings, had suddenly resolved themselves into a potent demand for expression. Miss Evans was sitting on one of the Hebrew tombs, her chin on her hand, her elbow on her knee, watching the broken horizon. I was stretched on the grass on my side, leaning on my elbow and on my hand, with my eyes on her face. She bent her own eyes and encountered mine; we neither of us spoke or moved, but exchanged a long steady regard; after which her eyes returned to the distance. What was her feeling toward me? Had she any sense of my emotion or of any answering trouble in her own wonderful heart? Suppose she should deny me: should I suffer, would I persist? At any rate, I should have struck a blow for love. Suppose she were to accept me; would my joy be any greater than in the mere translation of my heart-beats? Did I in truth long merely for a bliss which should be of that hour and that hour alone? I was conscious of an immense respect for the woman beside me. I was unconscious of the least desire even to touch the hem of her garment as it lay on the grass, touching my own. After all, it was but ten days that I had known her. How little I really knew of her! how little else than her beauty and her wit! How little she knew of me, of my vast out-lying, unsentimental, spiritual self! We knew hardly more of each other than had appeared in this narrow circle of our common impressions of Venice. And yet if into such a circle Love had forced his way, let him take his way! Let him widen the circle! Transcendent Venice! I rose to my feet with a violent movement, and walked ten steps away. I came back and flung myself again on the grass.

"The other day at Vicenza," I said, "I bought a picture."

"Ah? an 'original'?"

"No, a copy."

"From whom?"

"From you!"

She blushed. "What do you mean?"

"It was a little pretended Correggio; a Madonna and Child."

"Is it good?"

"No, it's rather poor."

"Why, then, did you buy it?"

"Because the Madonna looked singularly like you."

"I'm sorry, Mr. Brooke, you hadn't a better reason. I hope the picture was cheap."

"It was quite reason enough. I admire you more than any woman in the world."

She looked at me a moment, blushing again. "You don't know me."

"I have a suspicion of you. It's ground enough for admiration."

"O, don't talk about admiration. I'm tired of it all beforehand."

"Well, then," said I, "I'm in love."

"Not with me, I hope."

"With you, of course. With whom else?"

"Has it only just now occurred to you?"

"It has just occurred to me to say it."

Her blush had deepened a little; but a genuine smile came to its relief. "Poor Mr. Brooke!" she said.

"Poor Mr. Brooke indeed, if you take it in that way."

"You must forgive me if I doubt of your love."

"Why should you doubt?"

"Love, I fancy, doesn't come in just this way."

"It comes as it can. This is surely a very good way."

"I know it's a very pretty way, Mr. Brooke; Venice behind us, the Adriatic before us, these old Hebrew tombs! Its very prettiness makes me distrust it."

"Do you believe only in the love that is born in darkness and pain? Poor love! it has trouble enough, first and last. Allow it a little ease."

"Listen," said Miss Evans, after a pause. "It's not with me you're in love, but with that painted picture. All this Italian beauty and delight has thrown you into a romantic state of mind. You wish to make it perfect. I happen to be at hand, so you say, 'Go to, I'll fall in love.' And you fancy me, for the purpose, a dozen fine things that I'm not."

"I fancy you beautiful and good. I'm sorry to find you so dogmatic."

"You mustn't abuse me, or we shall be getting serious."

"Well," said I, "you can't prevent me from adoring you."

"I should be very sorry to. So long as you 'adore' me, we're safe! I can tell you better things than that I'm in love with you."

I looked at her impatiently. "For instance?"

She held out her hand. "I like you immensely. As for love, I'm in love with Venice."

"Well, I like Venice immensely, but I'm in love with you."

"In that way I am willing to leave it. Pray don't speak of it again to-day. But my poor father is probably wandering up to his knees in the sand."

I had been happy before, but I think I was still happier for the words I had spoken. I had cast them abroad at all events; my heart was richer by a sense of their possible fruition. We walked far along the beach. Mr. Evans was still with his friend.

"What is beyond that horizon?" said my companion.

"Greece, among other things."

"Greece! only think of it! Shall you never go there?"

I stopped short. "If you will believe what I say, Miss Evans, we may both go there." But for all answer she repeated her request that I should forbear. Before long, retracing our steps, we met Mr. Evans, who had parted with his friend, the latter having returned to Venice. He had arranged to start the next morning for Milan. We went back over the lagoon in the glow of the sunset, in a golden silence which suffered us to hear the far-off ripple in the wake of other gondolas, a golden clearness so perfect that the rosy flush on the marble palaces seemed as light and pure as the life-blood on the forehead of a sleeping child. There is no Venice like the Venice of that magical hour. For that brief period her ancient glory returns. The sky arches over her like a vast imperial canopy crowded with its clustering mysteries of light. Her whole aspect is one of unspotted splendor. No other city takes the crimson evanescence of day with such magnificent effect. The lagoon is sheeted with a carpet of fire. All torpid, pallid hues of marble are transmuted to a golden glow. The dead Venetian tone brightens and quickens into life and lustre, and the spectator's enchanted vision seems to rest on an embodied dream of the great painter who wrought his immortal reveries into the ceilings of the Ducal Palace.

It was not till the second day after this that I again saw Miss Evans. I went to the little church of San Cassiano, to see a famous Tintoretto, to which I had already made several vain attempts to obtain access. At the door in the little bustling *campo* which adjoins the church I found her standing expectant. A little boy, she told me, had gone for the sacristan and his key. Her father, she proceeded to explain, had suddenly been summoned to Milan by a telegram from Mr. Munson, the friend whom he had met at the Lido, who had suddenly been taken ill.

"And so you're going about alone? Do you think that's altogether proper? Why didn't you send for me?" I stood lost in wonder and admiration at the exquisite dignity of her self-support. I had heard of American girls doing such things; but I had yet to see them done.

"Do you think it less proper for me to go about alone than to send for you? Venice has seen so many worse improprieties that she'll forgive me mine."

The little boy arrived with the sacristan and his key, and we were ushered into the presence of Tintoretto's Crucifixion. This great picture is one of the greatest of the Venetian school. Tintoretto, the travelled reader will remember, has painted two masterpieces on this tremendous theme. The larger and more complex work is at the Scuola di San Rocco; the one of which I speak is small, simple, and sublime. It occupies the left side of the narrow choir of the shabby little church which we had entered, and is remarkable as being, with two or three exceptions, the best preserved work of its incomparable author. Never, in the whole range of art, I imagine, has so powerful an effect been produced by means so simple and select; never has the intelligent choice of means to an effect been pursued with such a refinement of perception. The picture offers to our sight the very central essence of the great tragedy which it depicts. There is no swooning Madonna, no consoling Magdalen, no mockery of contrast, no cruelty of an assembled host. We behold the silent summit of Calvary. To the right are the three crosses, that of the Saviour foremost. A ladder pitched against it supports a turbaned executioner, who bends downward to receive the sponge offered him by a comrade. Above the crest of the hill the helmets and spears of a line of soldiery complete the grimness of the scene. The reality of the picture is beyond all words: it is hard to say which is more impressive, the naked horror of the fact represented, or the sensible power of the artist. You breathe a silent prayer of thanks that you, for your part, are without the terrible clairvoyance of genius. We sat and looked at the picture in silence. The sacristan loitered about; but finally, weary of waiting, he retired to the *campo* without. I observed my companion; pale, motionless, oppressed, she evidently felt with poignant sympathy the commanding force of the work. At last I spoke to her; receiving no answer, I repeated my question. She rose to her feet and turned her face upon me, illumined with a vivid ecstasy of pity. Then passing me rapidly, she descended into the aisle of the church, dropped into a chair, and, burying her face in her hands, burst into an agony of sobs. Having allowed time for her feeling to expend itself, I went to her and recommended her not to let the day close on this painful emotion. "Come with me to the Ducal Palace," I said; "let us look at the Rape of Europa." But before departing we went back to our Tintoretto, and gave it another solemn half-hour. Miss Evans repeated aloud a dozen verses from St. Mark's Gospel.

"What is it here," I asked, "that has moved you most, the painter or the subject?"

"I suppose it's the subject. And you?"

"I'm afraid it's the painter."

We went to the Ducal Palace, and immediately made our way to that transcendent shrine of light and grace, the room which contains the masterpiece of Paul Veronese, and the Bacchus and Ariadne of his solemn comrade. I steeped myself with unprotesting joy in the gorgeous glow and salubrity of that radiant scene, wherein, against her bosky screen of immortal verdure, the rosy-footed, pearl-circled, nymph-flattered victim of a divine delusion rustles her lustrous satin against the ambrosial hide of bovine Jove. "It makes one think more agreeably of life," I said to my friend, "that such visions have blessed the eyes of men of mortal mould. What has been may be again. We may yet dream as brightly, and some few of us translate our dreams as freely."

"This, I think, is the brighter dream of the two," she answered, indicating the Bacchus and Ariadne. Miss Evans, on the whole, was perhaps right. In Tintoretto's picture there is no shimmer of drapery, no splendour of flowers and gems; nothing but the broad, bright glory of deep-toned sea and sky, and the shining purity and symmetry of deified human flesh. "What do you think," asked my companion, "of the painter of that tragedy at San Cassiano being also the painter of this dazzling idyl; of the great painter of darkness being also the great painter of light?"

"He was a colourist! Let us thank the great man, and be colourists too. To understand this Bacchus and Ariadne we ought to spend a long day on the lagoon, beyond sight of Venice. Will you come to-morrow to Torcello?" The proposition seemed to me audacious; I was conscious of blushing a little as I made it. Miss Evans looked at me and pondered. She then replied with great calmness that she preferred to wait for her father, the excursion being one that he would probably enjoy. "Will you come, then,— somewhere?" I asked.

Again she pondered. Suddenly her face brightened. "I should very much like to go to Padua. It would bore my poor father to go. I fancy he would thank you for taking me. I should be almost willing," she said with a smile, "to go alone."

It was easily arranged that on the morrow we should go for the day to Padua. Miss Evans was certainly an American to perfection. Nothing remained for me, as the good American which I aspired to be, but implicitly to respect her confidence. To Padua, by an early train, we accordingly went. The day stands out in my memory delightfully curious and rich. Padua is a wonderful little city. Miss Evans was an excellent walker, and, thanks to the broad arcades which cover the foot-ways in the streets, we rambled for hours in perpetual shade. We spent an hour at the famous church of St. Anthony, which boasts one of the richest and holiest shrines in all church-burdened Italy. The whole edifice is nobly and darkly ornate and picturesque, but the chapel of its patron saint—a wondrous combination of chiselled gold and silver and alabaster and perpetual flame—splendidly outshines and outshadows the rest. In all Italy, I think, the idea of palpable, material sanctity is nowhere more potently enforced.

"O, the Church, the Church!" murmured Miss Evans, as we stood contemplating.

"What a real pity," I said, "that we are not Catholics; that that dazzling monument is not something more to us than a mere splendid show! What a different thing this visiting of churches would be for us, if we occasionally felt the prompting to fall on our knees. I begin to grow ashamed of this perpetual attitude of bald curiosity. What a pleasant thing it must be, in such a church as this, for two good friends to say their prayers together!"

"*Ecco!*" said Miss Evans. Two persons had approached the glittering shrine,—a young woman of the middle class and a man of her own rank, some ten years older, dressed with a good deal of cheap elegance. The woman dropped on her knees; her companion fell back a few steps, and stood gazing idly at the chapel.

"Poor girl!" said my friend, "she believes; he doubts."

"He doesn't look like a doubter. He's a vulgar fellow. They're a betrothed pair, I imagine. She is very pretty." She had turned round and flung at her companion a liquid glance of entreaty. He appeared not to observe it; but in a few moments he slowly approached her, and bent a single knee at her side. When presently they rose to their feet, she passed her arm into his with a beautiful, unsuppressed lovingness. As they passed us, looking at us from the clear darkness of their Italian brows, I keenly envied them. "They are better off than we," I said. "Be they husband and wife, or lovers, or simply friends, we, I think, are rather vulgar beside them."

"My dear Mr. Brooke," said Miss Evans, "go by all means and say your prayers." And she walked away to the other side of the church. Whether I obeyed her injunction or not, I feel under no obligation to report. I rejoined her at the beautiful frescoed chapel in the opposite transept. She was sitting listlessly turning over the leaves of her Murray. "I suppose," she said, after a few moments, "that nothing is more vulgar than to make a noise about having been called vulgar. But really, Mr. Brooke, don't call me so again. I have been of late so fondly fancying I am not vulgar."

"My dear Miss Evans, you are—"

"Come, nothing vulgar!"

"You're divine!"

"*A la bonne heure!* Divinities needn't pray. They are prayed to."

I have no space and little power to enumerate and describe the various curiosities of Padua. I think we saw them all. We left the best, however, for the last, and repaired in the late afternoon, after dining fraternally at a restaurant, to the Chapel of Giotto. This little empty church, standing unshaded and forlorn in the homely market-garden which was once a Roman arena, offers one of the deepest lessons of Italian travel. Its four walls are covered, almost from base to ceiling, with that wonderful series of dramatic paintings which usher in the golden prime of Italian art. I had been so ill-informed as to fancy that to talk about Giotto was to make more or less of a fool of one's self, and that he was the especial property of the mere sentimentalists of criticism. But you no sooner cross the threshold of that little ruinous temple—a mere empty shell, but coated as with the priceless substance of fine pearls and vocal with a murmured eloquence as from the infinite of art—than you perceive with whom you have to deal: a complete painter of the very strongest sort. In one respect, assuredly, Giotto has never been surpassed,—in the art of presenting a story. The amount of dramatic expression compressed into those quaint little scenic squares would equip a thousand later masters. How, beside him, they seem to fumble and grope and trifle! And he, beside them, how direct he seems, how essential, how masculine! What a solid simplicity, what an immediate purity and grace! The exhibition suggested to my friend and me more wise reflections than we had the skill to utter. "Happy, happy art," we said, as we seemed to see it beneath Giotto's hand tremble and thrill and sparkle, almost, with a presentiment of its immense career, "for the next two hundred years what a glorious felicity will be yours!" The chapel door stood open into the sunny corn-field, and the lazy litter of verdure enclosed by the crumbling oval of Roman masonry. A loutish boy who had come with the key lounged on a bench, awaiting tribute, and gazing at us as we gazed. The ample light flooded the inner precinct, and lay hot upon the coarse, pale surface of the painted wall. There seemed an irresistible pathos in such a combination of shabbiness and beauty. I thought of this subsequently at the beautiful Museum at Bologna, where mediocrity is so richly enshrined. Nothing that we had yet seen together had filled us with so deep a sense of enjoyment. We stared, we laughed, we wept almost, we raved with a decent delight. We went over the little compartments one by one: we lingered and returned and compared; we studied; we melted together in unanimous homage. At last the light began to fade and the little saintly figures to grow quaint and terrible in the gathering dusk. The loutish boy had transferred himself significantly to the door-post: we lingered for a farewell glance.

"Mr. Brooke," said my companion, "we ought to learn from all this to be *real*; real even as Giotto is real; to discriminate between genuine and factitious sentiment; between the substantial and the trivial; between the essential and the superfluous; sentiment and sentimentality."

"You speak," said I, "with appalling wisdom and truth. You strike a chill to my heart of hearts."

She spoke unsmiling, with a slightly contracted brow and an apparent sense of effort. She blushed as I gazed at her.

"Well," she said, "I'm extremely glad to have been here. Good, wise Giotto! I should have liked to know you.—Nay, let me pay the boy." I saw the piece she put into his hand; he was stupefied by its magnitude.

"We shall not have done Padua," I said, as we left the garden, "unless we have been to the Caffè Pedrocchi. Come to the Caffè Pedrocchi. We have more than an hour before our train,—time to eat an ice." So we drove to the Caffè Pedrocchi, the most respectable café in the world; a café monumental, scholastic, classical.

We sat down at one of the tables on the cheerful external platform, which is washed by the gentle tide of Paduan life. When we had finished our ices, Miss Evans graciously allowed me a cigar. How it came about I hardly remember, but, prompted by some happy accident of talk, and gently encouraged perhaps by my smoke-wreathed quietude, she lapsed, with an exquisite feminine reserve, into a delicate autobiographical strain. For a moment she became egotistical; but with a modesty, a dignity, a lightness of touch which filled my eyes with admiring tears. She spoke of her home, her family, and the few events of her life. She had lost her mother in her early years; her two sisters had married young; she and her father were equally united by affection and habit. Upon one theme she touched, in regard to which I should be at loss to say whether her treatment told more, by its frankness, of our friendship, or, by its reticence, of her modesty. She spoke of having been engaged, and of having lost her betrothed in the Civil War. She made no story of it; but I felt from her words that she had tasted of sorrow. Having finished my cigar, I was proceeding to light another. She drew out her watch. Our train was to leave at eight o'clock. It was now a quarter past. There was no later evening train.

The reader will understand that I tell the simple truth when I say that our situation was most disagreeable and that we were deeply annoyed. "Of course," said I, "you are utterly disgusted."

She was silent. "I am extremely sorry," she said, at last, just vanquishing a slight tremor in her voice.

"Murray says the hotel is good," I suggested.

She made no answer. Then, rising to her feet, "Let us go immediately," she said. We drove to the principal inn and bespoke our rooms. Our want of luggage provoked, of course, a certain amount of visible surprise. This, however, I fancy, was speedily merged in a more flattering emotion, when my companion, having communed with the chambermaid, sent her forth with a list of purchases.

We separated early. "I hope," said I, as I bade her good night, "that you will be fairly comfortable."

She had recovered her equanimity. "I have no doubt of it."

"Good night."

"Good night." Thank God, I silently added, for the dignity of American women. Knowing to what suffering a similar accident would have subjected a young girl of the orthodox European training, I felt devoutly grateful that among my own people a woman and her reputation are more indissolubly one. And yet I was unable to detach myself from my old-world associations effectually enough not to wonder whether, after all, Miss Evans's calmness might not be the simple calmness of despair. The miserable words rose to my lips, "Is she compromised?" If she were, of course, as far as I was concerned, there was but one possible sequel to our situation.

We met the next morning at breakfast. She assured me that she had slept, but I doubted it. I myself had not closed my eyes,—not from the excitement of vanity. Owing partly, I suppose, to a natural reaction against our continuous talk on the foregoing day, our return to Venice was attended with a good deal of silence. I wondered whether it was a mere fancy that Miss Evans was pensive, appealing, sombre. As we entered the gondola to go from the railway station to the Hotel Danieli, she asked me to request the gondoliers to pass along the Canalezzo rather than through the short cuts of the smaller canals. "I feel as if I were coming home," she said, as we floated beneath the lovely façade of the Ca' Doro. Suddenly she laid her hand on my arm. "It seems to me," she said, "that I should like to stop for Mrs. L——," and she mentioned the wife of the American Consul. "I have promised to show her some jewelry. This is a particularly good time. I shall ask her to come home with me." We stopped accordingly at the American Consulate. Here we found, on inquiry, to my great regret, that the Consul and his wife had gone for a week to the Lake of Como. For a moment my companion meditated. Then, "To the hotel," she said with decision. Our arrival attracted apparently little notice. I went with Miss Evans to the door of her father's sitting-room, where we met a servant, who informed us with inscrutable gravity that Monsieur had returned the evening before, but that he had gone out after breakfast and had not reappeared.

"Poor father," she said. "It was very stupid of me not to have left a note for him." I urged that our absence for the night was not to have been foreseen, and that Mr. Evans had in all likelihood very plausibly explained it. I withdrew with a hand-shake and permission to return in the evening.

I went to my hotel and slept, a long, sound, dreamless sleep. In the afternoon I called my gondola, and went over to the Lido. I crossed to the outer shore and sought the spot where a few days before I had lain at the feet of Charlotte Evans. I stretched myself on the grass and fancied her present. To say that I *thought* would be to say at once more and less than the literal truth. I was in a tremulous glow of feeling. I listened to the muffled rupture of the tide, vaguely conscious of my beating heart. Was I or was I not in love? I was able to settle nothing. I wandered musingly further and further from the point. Every now and then, with a deeper pulsation of the heart, I would return to it, but only to start afresh and follow some wire-drawn thread of fancy to a nebulous goal of doubt. That she was a most lovely woman seemed to me of all truths the truest, but it was a hard-featured fact of the senses rather than a radiant mystery of faith. I felt that I was not possessed by a passion; perhaps I was incapable of passion. At last, weary of self-bewilderment, I left the spot and wandered beside the sea. It seemed to speak more musingly than ever of the rapture of motion and freedom. Beyond the horizon was Greece, beyond and below was the wondrous Southern world which blooms about the margin of the Midland Sea. To marry, somehow, meant to abjure all this, and in the prime of youth and manhood to sink into obscurity and care. For a moment there stirred in my heart a feeling of anger and pain. Perhaps, after all, I *was* in love!

I went straight across the lagoon to the Hotel Danieli, and as I approached it I became singularly calm and collected. From below I saw Miss Evans alone on her balcony, watching the sunset. She received me with perfect friendly composure. Her father had again gone out, but she had told him of my coming, and he was soon to return. He had not been painfully alarmed at her absence, having learned through a chambermaid, to whom she had happened to mention her intention, that she had gone for the day to Padua.

"And what have you been doing all day?" I asked.

"Writing letters,—long, tiresome, descriptive letters. I have also found a volume of Hawthorne, and have been reading 'Rappaccini's Daughter.' You know the scene is laid in Padua." And what had I been doing?

Whether I was in a passion of love or not, I was enough in love to be very illogical. I was disappointed, Heaven knows why! that she should have been able to spend her time in this wholesome fashion. "I have been at the Lido, at the Hebrew tombs, where we sat the other day, thinking of what you told me there.'

"What I told you?"

"That you liked me immensely."

She smiled; but now that she smiled, I fancied I saw in the movement of her face an undercurrent of pain. Had the peace of her heart been troubled? "You needn't have gone so far away to think of it."

"It's very possible," I said, "that I shall have to think of it, in days to come, farther away still."

"Other places, Mr. Brooke, will bring other thoughts."

"Possibly. This place has brought that one." At what prompting it was that I continued I hardly know; I *would* tell her that I loved her. "I value it beyond all other thoughts."

"I do like you, Mr. Brooke. Let it rest there."

"It may rest there for you. It can't for me. It begins there! Don't refuse to understand me."

She was silent. Then, bending her eyes on me, "Perhaps," she said, "I understand you too well."

"O, in Heaven's name, don't play at coldness and scepticism!"

She dropped her eyes gravely on a bracelet which she locked and unlocked on her wrist. "I think," she said, without raising them, "you had better leave Venice." I was about to reply, but the door opened and Mr. Evans came in. From is hard, grizzled brow he looked at us in turn; then, greeting me with an extended hand, he spoke to his daughter.

"I have forgotten my cigar-case. Be so good as to fetch it from my dressing-table."

For a moment Miss Evans hesitated and cast upon him a faint protesting glance. Then she lightly left the room. He stood holding my hand, with a very sensible firmness, with his eyes on mine. Then, laying his other hand heavily on my shoulder, "Mr. Brooke," he said, "I believe you are an honest man."

"I hope so," I answered.

He paused, and I felt his steady gray eyes. "How the devil," he said, "came you to be left at Padua?"

"The explanation is a very simple one. Your daughter must have told you."

"I have thought best to talk very little to my daughter about it."

"Do you regard it, Mr. Evans," I asked, "as a very serious calamity?"

"I regard it as an infernally disagreeable thing. It seems that the whole hotel is talking about it. There is a little beast of an Italian down stairs—"

"Your daughter, I think, was not seriously discomposed."

"My daughter is a d—d proud woman!"

"I can assure you that my esteem for her is quite equal to your own."

"What does that mean, Mr. Brooke?" I was about to answer, but Miss Evans reappeared. Her father, as he took his cigar-case from her, looked at her intently, as if he were on the point of speaking, but the words remained on his lips, and, declaring that he would be back in half an hour, he left the room.

His departure was followed by a long silence.

"Miss Evans," I said, at last, "will you be my wife?"

She looked at me with a certain firm resignation. "Do you *feel* that, Mr. Brooke? Do you know what you ask?"

"Most assuredly."

"Will you rest content with my answer?"

"It depends on what your answer is."

She was silent.

"I should like to know what my father said to you in my absence."

"You had better learn from himself."

"I think I know. Poor father!"

"But you give me no answer," I rejoined, after a pause.

She frowned a little. "Mr. Brooke," she said, "you disappoint me."

"Well, I'm sorry. Don't revenge yourself by disappointing me."

"I fancied that I had answered your proposal; that I had, at least, anticipated it, the other day at the Lido."

"O, that was very good for the other day; but do give me something different now."

"I doubt of your being more in earnest to-day than then."

"It seems to suit you wonderfully well to doubt! "

"I thank you for the honour of your proposal: but I can't be your wife, Mr. Brooke."

"That's the answer with which you ask me to remain satisfied!"

"Let me repeat what I said just now. You had better leave Venice, otherwise we must leave it."

"Ah, that's easy to say!"

"You mustn't think me unkind or cynical. You have done your duty."

"My duty—what duty?"

"Come," she said, with a beautiful blush and the least attempt at a smile, "you imagine that I have suffered an injury by my being left with you at Padua. I don't believe in such injuries."

"No more do I."

"Then there is even less wisdom than before in your proposal. But I strongly suspect that if we had not missed the train at Padua, you would not have made it. There is an idea of reparation in it.— O Sir!" And she shook her head with a deepening smile.

"If I had flattered myself that it lay in my power to do you an injury," I replied, "I should now be rarely disenchanted. As little almost as to do you a benefit!"

"You have loaded me with benefits. I thank you from the bottom of my heart. I may be very unreasonable, but if I had doubted of my having to decline your offer three days ago, I should have quite ceased to doubt this evening."

"You are an excessively proud woman. I can tell you that."

"Possibly. But I'm not as proud as you think. I believe in my common sense."

"I wish that for five minutes you had a grain of imagination!"

"If only for the same five minutes you were without it. You have too much, Mr. Brooke. You imagine you love me."

"Poor fool that I am!"

"You imagine that I'm charming. I assure you I'm not in the least. Here in Venice I have not been myself at all. You should see me at home."

"Upon my word, Miss Evans, you remind me of a German philosopher. I have not the least objection to seeing you at home."

"Don't fancy that I think lightly of your offer. But we have been living, Mr. Brooke, in poetry. Marriage is stern prose. Do let me bid you farewell!"

I took up my hat. "I shall go from here to Rome and Naples," I said. "I must leave Florence for the last. I shall write you from Rome and of course see you there."

"I hope not. I had rather not meet you again in Italy. It perverts our dear good old American truth!"

"Do you really propose to bid me a final farewell?"

She hesitated a moment. "When do you return home?"

"Some time in the spring."

"Very well. If a year hence, in America, you are still of your present mind, I shall not decline to see you. I feel very safe! If you are not of your present mind, of course I shall be still more happy. Farewell." She put out her hand; I took it.

"Beautiful, wonderful woman!" I murmured

"That's rank poetry! Farewell!"

I raised her hand to my lips and released it in silence. At this point Mr. Evans reappeared, considering apparently that his half-hour was up. "Are you going?" he asked.

"Yes. I start to-morrow for Rome."

"The deuce! Daughter, when are we to go?"

She moved her hand over her forehead, and a sort of nervous tremor seemed to pass through her limbs. "O, you must take me home!" she said. "I'm horribly homesick!" She flung her arms round his neck and buried her head on his shoulder. Mr. Evans with a movement of his head dismissed me.

At the top of the staircase, however, he overtook me. "You made your offer!" And he passed his arm into mine.

"Yes!"

"And she refused you?" I nodded. He looked at me, squeezing my arm. "By Jove, sir, if she had accepted—"

" Well!" said I, stopping.

"Why, it wouldn't in the least have suited me! Not that I don't esteem you. The whole house shall see it." With his arm in mine we passed down stairs, through the hall, to the landing-place, where he called his own gondola and requested me to use it. He bade me farewell with a kindly hand-shake, and the assurance that I was too "nice a fellow not to keep as a friend."

I think, on the whole, that my uppermost feeling was a sense of freedom and relief. It seemed to me on my journey to Florence that I had started afresh, and was regarding things with less of nervous rapture than before, but more of sober insight. Of Miss Evans I forbade myself to think. In my deepest heart I admitted the truth, the partial truth at least, of her assertion of the unreality of my love. The reality I believed would come. The way to hasten its approach was, meanwhile, to study, to watch, to observe,—doubtless even to enjoy. I certainly enjoyed Florence and the three days I spent there. But I shall not attempt to deal with Florence in a parenthesis. I subsequently saw that divine little city under circumstances which peculiarly coloured and shaped it. In Rome, to begin with, I spent a week and went down to Naples, dragging the heavy Roman chain which she rivets about your limbs forever. In Naples I discovered the real South—the Southern South,—in art, in nature, in man, and the least bit in woman. A German lady, an old kind friend, had given me a letter to a Neapolitan lady

whom she assured me she held in high esteem. The Signora B——
was at Sorrento, where I presented my letter. It seemed to me that
"esteem" was not exactly the word; but the Signora B—— was
charming. She assured me on my first visit that she was a "true
Neapolitan," and I think, on the whole, she was right. She told me
that I was a true German, but in this she was altogether wrong. I
spent four days in her house; on one of them we went to Capri,
where the Signora had an infant—her only one—at nurse. We saw
the Blue Grotto, the Tiberian ruins, the tarantella and the infant,
and returned late in the evening by moonlight. The Signora sang
on the water in a magnificent contralto. As I looked upward at
Northern Italy, it seemed, in contrast, a cold, dark hyperborean
clime, a land of order, conscience, and virtue. How my heart went
out to that brave, rich, compact little Verona! How there Nature
seemed to have mixed her colours with potent oil, instead of as
here with crystalline water, drawn though it was from the Neapolitan Bay! But in Naples, too, I pursued my plan of vigilance and
study. I spent long mornings at the Museum and learned to know
Pompei; I wrote once to Miss Evans, about the statues in the
Museum, without a word of wooing, but received no answer. It
seemed to me that I returned to Rome a wiser man. It was the
middle of October when I reached it. Unless Mr. Evans had altered
his programme, he would at this moment be passing down to
Naples.

A fortnight elapsed without my hearing of him, during which
I was in the full fever of initiation into Roman wonders. I had been
introduced to an old German archæologist, with whom I spent a
series of memorable days in the exploration of ruins and the study
of the classical topography. I thought, I lived, I ate and drank, in
Latin, and German Latin at that. But I remember with especial
delight certain long lonely rides on the Campagna. The weather
was perfect. Nature seemed only to slumber, ready to wake far
on the hither side of wintry death. From time to time, after a
passionate gallop, I would pull up my horse on the slope of some
pregnant mound and embrace with the ecstasy of quickened
senses the tragical beauty of the scene; strain my ear to the soft low
silence, pity the dark dishonoured plain, watch the heavens come

rolling down in tides of light, and breaking in waves of fire against the massive stillness of temples and tombs. The aspect of all this sunny solitude and haunted vacancy used to fill me with a mingled sense of exaltation and dread. There were moments when my fancy swept that vast funereal desert with passionate curiosity and desire, moments when it felt only its potent sweetness and its high historic charm. But there were other times when the air seemed so heavy with the exhalation of unburied death, so bright with sheeted ghosts, that I turned short about and galloped back to the city. One afternoon after I had indulged in one of these super-sensitive flights on the Campagna, I betook myself to St. Peter's. It was shortly before the opening of the recent Council, and the city was filled with foreign ecclesiastics, the increase being of course especially noticeable in the churches. At St. Peter's they were present in vast numbers; great armies encamped in prayer on the marble plains of its pavement: an inexhaustible physiognomical study. Scattered among them were squads of little tonsured neophytes, clad in scarlet, marching and counter-marching, and ducking and flapping, like poor little raw recruits for the heavenly host. I had never before, I think, received an equal impression of the greatness of this church of churches, or, standing beneath the dome, beheld such a vision of erected altitude,—of the builded sublime. I lingered awhile near the brazen image of St. Peter, observing the steady procession of his devotees. Near me stood a lady in mourning, watching with a weary droop of the head the grotesque deposition of kisses. A peasant-woman advanced with the file of the faithful and lifted up her little girl to the well-worn toe. With a sudden movement of impatience the lady turned away, so that I saw her face to face. She was strikingly pale, but as her eyes met mine the blood rushed into her cheeks. This lonely mourner was Miss Evans. I advanced to her with an outstretched hand. Before she spoke I had guessed at the truth.

"You're in sorrow and trouble!"

She nodded, with a look of simple gravity.

"Why in the world haven't you written to me?"

"There was no use. I seem to have sufficed to myself."

"Indeed, you have not sufficed to yourself. You are pale and worn; you look wretchedly." She stood silent, looking about her with an air of vague unrest. "I have as yet heard nothing," I said. "Can you speak of it?"

"O, Mr. Brooke!" she said with a simple sadness that went to my heart. I drew her hand through my arm and led her to the extremity of the left transept of the church. We sat down together, and she told me of her father's death. It had happened ten days before, in consequence of a severe apoplectic stroke. He had been ill but a single day, and had remained unconscious from first to last. The American physician had been extremely kind, and had relieved her of all care and responsibility. His wife had strongly urged her to come and stay in their house, until she should have determined what to do; but she had preferred to remain at her hotel. She had immediately furnished herself with an attendant in the person of a French maid, who had come with her to the church and was now at confession. At first she had wished greatly to leave Rome, but now that the first shock of grief had passed away she found it suited her mood to linger on from day to day. "On the whole," she said, with a sober smile, "I have got through it all rather easily than otherwise. The common cares and necessities of life operate strongly to interrupt and dissipate one's grief. I shall feel my loss more when I get home again." Looking at her while she talked, I found a pitiful difference between her words and her aspect. Her pale face, her wilful smile, her spiritless gestures, spoke most forcibly of loneliness and weakness. Over this gentle weakness and dependence I secretly rejoiced; I felt in my heart an immense uprising of pity,—of the pity that goes hand in hand with love. At its bidding I hastily, vaguely sketched a magnificent scheme of devotion and protection.

"When I think of what you have been through," I said, "my heart stands still for very tenderness. Have you made any plans?" She shook her head with such a perfection of helplessness that I broke into a sort of rage of compassion: "One of the last things your father said to me was that you are a very proud woman."

She coloured faintly. "I may have been! But there is not among the most abject peasants who stand kissing St. Peter's foot a creature more bowed in humility than I."

"How did you expect to make that weary journey home?"

She was silent a moment and her eyes filled with tears. "O, don't cross-question me, Mr. Brooke!" she softly cried; "I expected nothing. I was waiting for my stronger self."

"Perhaps your stronger self has come." She rose to her feet as if she had not heard me, and went forward to meet her maid. This was a decent, capable-looking person, with a great deal of apparent deference of manner. As I rejoined them, Miss Evans prepared to bid me farewell. "You haven't yet asked me to come and see you," I said.

"Come, but not too soon?"

"What do you call too soon? This evening?"

"Come to-morrow." She refused to allow me to go with her to her carriage. I followed her, however, at a short interval, and went as usual to my restaurant to dine. I remember that my dinner cost me ten francs,—it usually cost me five. Afterwards, as usual, I adjourned to the Caffè Greco, where I met my German archae-ologist. He discoursed with even more than his wonted sagacity and eloquence; but at the end of half an hour he rapped his fist on the table and asked me what the deuce was the matter; he would wager I hadn't heard a word of what he said.

I went forth the next morning into the Roman streets, doubt-ing heavily of my being able to exist until evening without seeing Miss Evans. I felt, however, that it was due to her to make the effort. To help myself through the morning, I went into the Borghese Gallery. The great treasure of this collection is a certain master-piece of Titian. I entered the room in which it hangs by the door facing the picture. The room was empty, save that before the great Titian, beside the easel of an absent copyist, stood a young woman in mourning. This time, in spite of her averted head, I immediately knew her and noiselessly approached her. The picture is one of the finest of its admirable author,—rich and simple and brilliant with the true Venetian fire. It unites the charm of an air of latent symbolism with a steadfast splendour and solid perfection of design. Beside a low sculptured well sit two young and beautiful women: one richly clad, and full of mild dignity and repose; the other with unbound hair, naked, ungirdled by a great reverted mantle of Venetian purple, and radiant with the frankest physical sweetness and grace. Between them a little winged cherub bends forward and thrusts his chubby arm into the well. The picture glows with the inscrutable chemistry of the prince of colourists.

"Does it remind you of Venice?" I said, breaking a long silence, during which she had not noticed me.

She turned and her face seemed bright with reflected colour. We spoke awhile of common things; she had come alone. "What an emotion, for one who has loved Venice," she said, "to meet a Titian in other lands."

"They call it," I answered—and as I spoke my heart was in my throat,—"a representation of Sacred and Profane Love. The name perhaps roughly expresses its meaning. The serious, stately woman is the likeness, one may say, of love as an experience,—the gracious, impudent goddess of love as a sentiment; this of the passion that fancies, the other of the passion that knows." And as I spoke I passed my arm, in its strength, around her waist. She let her head sink on my shoulders and looked up into my eyes.

"One may stand for the love I denied," she said; "and the other—"

"The other," I murmured, "for the love which, with this kiss, you accept." I drew her arm into mine, and before the envious eyes that watched us from gilded casements we passed through the gallery and left the palace. We went that afternoon to the Pamfili-Doria Villa. Saying just now that my stay in Florence was peculiarly coloured by circumstances, I meant that I was there with my wife.

Achevé d'imprimer sur Roto-Page par l'Imprimerie Floch à Mayenne, le 10 janvier 2005.
Dépôt légal : janvier 2005 - N° d'impression : 61961 - ISBN : 2-84304-287-9
Imprimé en France